GOOD QUESTION

GOOD
QUESTION

By V.R. Lyons

Matador
9 Priory Business Park,
Wistow Road, Kibworth Beauchamp,
Leicestershire, LE8 0RX
Tel: 0116 279 2299
Email: books@troubador.co.uk
Web: www.troubador.co.uk/matador
Twitter: @matadorbooks

ISBN 978 1838590 130

British Library Cataloguing in Publication Data.
A catalogue record for this book is available from the British Library.

Printed and bound in Great Britain by 4edge Limited
Typeset in 11pt Sabon MT by Troubador Publishing Ltd, Leicester, UK

Matador is an imprint of Troubador Publishing Ltd

To all those who help.

Thanks

I give great thanks to my family, Roberta, David and Tony, for 50 years (so far) of support and help through all sorts.

In writing this book I not only thank my family but also Graeme, Pat and Ian for suggestions, technical help and a good sense of direction.

PREQUEL

"Look, I told you yesterday, if you don't return that money you'll end up all twistifuddled. Get him in the car."

*

Terry had woken in much the same pain as he had felt when he fell asleep. He'd desperately tried to be tidy whilst he'd showered and dressed. He felt that somehow he'd brought something bad to Sue and Jeff's house and he didn't want to make things worse by leaving blood everywhere. Everything hurt afterwards but, just then, the hunger screamed louder. Painfully, he had made himself some tea and toast, but only took one bite before the back door smashed open.

In his rough state he barely had a chance to move before three blokes strode through the kitchen and into the dining room, looked around, grabbed him and shoved him back into the chair he was trying to get out of.

They were clearly blokes who didn't have to work hard at being called ugly and had the size to get what they wanted without words. As soon as he had been sat down he had a chance to look around and saw a fourth man walking out of the kitchen door. The first thing he noticed was the same smart shoes that had been in charge of the gang that had beaten him up the day before.

As Terry looked up he saw a surprising face above the well-dressed body. Then, with a voice that Terry felt he knew but didn't know, the man started talking.

"What was it about our message yesterday that you did not understand, Terry? You have taken money that does not belong to you and you need to give it back."

After a moment of trying to work the situation out, Terry replied.

"Look, you didn't exactly give me a chance to say anything yesterday but I don't know what you're on about," Terry said, still in confusion but somehow managing to keep a calm head. "I haven't taken any money."

"I wonder if any guilty people have ever just turned around and said, 'Fair cop, it was me, guv'."

"Well, this time it wasn't me. I don't know who you've got me mixed up with but you're going to put a lot of effort into hurting the wrong person."

Terry's normal way of keeping his feet firmly planted on the ground was somehow stopping him from giving in to the panicky voice that was starting to be heard somewhere inside his head. He knew that panicking would not get him anywhere, so he managed to stay level.

"The gentleman who is paying us knows it was you and we have no reason not to believe him. So, please just make everybody's life easier, tell us where it is, and we can all go back to whatever we were doing before. My boys here are going to miss their favourite quiz show."

"How many times do I have to say it? I've barely got any money of my own, let alone anybody else's."

The well-shod boss man looked up at the guy behind Terry, who squeezed hard on Terry's shoulder, creating a stabbing sensation in his broken rib. Terry grimaced with pain but stopped himself crying out.

"My boys know how to hurt people and they know what they did to you yesterday, so this is going to get very unpleasant very quickly. Before we mess up everybody's day I'll give you one last chance. Where is it?"

Terry just looked up blankly, shaking his head.

"Look, I told you yesterday…"

Terry didn't even listen to the rest of the threat or the command that followed and, before he knew it, two of the ugly blokes had grabbed him by an arm each and forced him out of the front door.

On the front path, one of his captors lost his footing on the gravel and loosened his grip on Terry's arm. Terry snatched his arm away and used it to try to push the other man away from him. Unfortunately for Terry, both of his unwanted companions regained their footing and grabbed his arms even tighter. They left the gravel disturbed and forcibly marched him to their car, where they folded him painfully into the boot.

Part I

———————

WHO?

Present Day

1

Early May

I know why but, really, WHY? Sue plaintively asked herself as she lugged her tired body towards their house in the May drizzle.

When she had finally pulled up the dark blue Vauxhall Corsa, Sue was relieved that she'd managed the parallel parking job in the one small space available on their terraced side road. When the houses had been built, for local steel factory workers at the very beginning of the 20th century, cars had only just been invented and nobody had thought that that class would have such things as cars. As a result, the roads weren't designed to cope with even one car per household, most of which had to be a similar compact size to stand any chance of fitting in. Just finding a space was always a game of chance, and of course the one she found was at least 400 yards from their house, almost at the end of the road. So, Sue and Jeff grabbed all of their bags so they could do it in one trip. The drizzle seemed to make the walk longer. It was that annoying steady spray-like 'in-your-face' stuff, not hard enough to call proper rain, but it got them wet nonetheless.

It may have been starting to get dark on this late May evening but they were happy to see that their neighbour's precious Geisha-Red Azalea was starting to come out with its large bright flowers. Most of the now-gentrified houses were owned by professional types who were too busy to do anything but the most basic of gardening. There was a lot of gravel, some hard paving and quite a few weeds in most of the front yards. Jeanette, on the other hand, their very likeable local accountant neighbour, still cared deeply about her potted azalea and would tell anyone who stood still long enough all about it. The light from the living room glistened on the drops of drizzle on the petals. Sue wasn't willing to think of them as raindrops. They reminded her too much of that cheery line about raindrops on roses from... *What was that film?* Nothing about this kind of weather felt cheery.

Of course, after two weeks away there was a fair collection of post on the floor when they opened their front door, mostly recyclable junk, with a few bills. As soon as they'd put their bags down, Sue picked up the post and Jeff moved close behind her and put his arms around her.

"Welcome home, Mrs Mead," he said with a gentle squeeze and a contented smile.

She squeezed his arms and smiled, mentally reminding herself that regrets on re-joining the real world after a holiday were normal and, really, everything was as it should be.

*

"Do you have time for some toast?" Jeff asked.

"I know I should but I'll be late if I do. Being late on your first day back after your holiday never looks good," Sue replied.

She straightened her smart pale-brown high-street suit, grabbed her coat and handbag and started for the door. She had already checked herself in the long bathroom mirror whilst she'd put her shoulder-length mousy-blonde hair in its usual ponytail, so she knew she looked OK. Her very ample brain was what was needed at work but she always made time to make sure her look was also a good one. She was happy that her five feet, three inch slim build suited the straight skirt, shaped white blouse and tailored jacket. At that height she appreciated the extra inch and a half the smart Mary Jane shoes gave her. She knew her day would take her all over the office, so it made sense not to go too crazy with heel height, but that bit extra was appreciated.

"Don't forget the goodies!" Jeff called, and Sue did a swift U-turn, grabbed the traditional holiday treats for her colleagues, planted a grateful kiss on the top of her husband's irresistibly soft dark-brown hair and headed out of the door.

As she stepped out into their front yard, Sue knew she had the worst of the rush hour traffic to deal with to get to work so she couldn't hang around. The street was practically empty of commuter cars by that point but Jeanette was still in her front yard tending to her azalea. She was obviously on her way to work, given the care she was taking not to get her suit dirty, so she and Sue exchanged 'good morning's before going their separate ways.

As she headed towards her car Sue quickly called back to Jeanette.

"It's looking lovely!"

"Thanks!" Jeanette called back.

Back in their house, Jeff grinned at his wife's hurriedness and turned back to his toast and the paper. He'd been able to book the morning off so he spread a bit more jam on his toast and spent the morning unpacking and sorting out some stuff on his laptop. When he was good and ready, he picked up his jacket and his holiday treats, turned the alarm on and lights off and headed for the bus stop. The trade-off for having the morning off was not having the car and having to mess about with buses, but he was happy. Of course, he was fully aware that there would be a small revolution if he failed to return with holiday goodies. He and Sue both worked for Cuthbert's national supermarket chain, in equally matched management roles, but Jeff knew that the whole company's success depended on the smooth running of his IT department, and that in turn depended on the plentiful supply of tea and holiday goodies.

*

"Welsh cakes, again! Do you ever do original?"

"What's wrong with Welsh cakes? They always seem to go fast enough, so I thought everyone liked them. And they're one of the things our beloved 'local in every way' Cuthbert's Supermarket doesn't sell outside of Wales."

"We do enjoy them, it's just that you always seem to come back with them. A bit of variety would be nice. They do make other things in Wales, you know."

"Of course I know. I just get what I know you all like, especially as we managed to get those lovely ones from that little bakery. Trust me, I'll start to open these up and the gannets will be here before they hit the plate."

That whole conversation between Sue and Kat, her department's team administrator and, for many years, her best friend, might have been taken seriously by anyone who hadn't seen the sarcastic grins on both their faces. They both knew their colleagues very well and each other even better.

Kat and Sue had actually started with Cuthbert's service centre on the same day nearly fifteen years earlier. Sue was taken on as a twenty-four-year-old trainee customer services telephone operator, ready to ask sensible questions and learn the business well enough to answer any phone queries that came in. Even though she'd never finished university, she was clearly a very smart woman with an inquisitive mind. She was rarely satisfied when things weren't as good as they could be and very quickly made suggestions for the best way of doing her job. When she'd asked why they had to transfer through so many parts of the IT system to find a customer's information, this had led to direct conversations with the IT department – and some other interesting improvements to her life. The constant questioning could have made her look arrogant, but she had such a friendly way about her, with her ideas always being evidence-based and right, and appreciated by her boss, Gina.

She moved steadily through the ranks, always becoming the best she could be at any job before moving up. At every step she worked closely with the teams around her, and by the time she became assistant service branch manager she knew the business, the people who worked there and their potential inside and out.

Kat, coincidentally also twenty-four, started out as a fairly junior office assistant. Her job was to make sure the service centre staff had whatever they needed to do their jobs properly. This could be anything from good strong coffee in the mornings to keeping the stationery cupboard properly stocked.

The job started out being pretty mundane, but what she really liked was how much she was appreciated. Right from its formation, Cuthbert's philosophy was based on treating everyone with equal respect, and this carried on through the years and through all departments. They all knew that everyone was not only helping to get the job done but getting it done well. Of course, the levels of appreciation went up when Kat provided tea or coffee, to personal preference, when it was most needed.

Kat's career path was pretty much as steady as Sue's, and by the time she eventually became office manager she had also become one of those essential colleagues without whom the department just wouldn't run. She also acted as Sue's assistant when needed, which, given that they were both very efficient, wasn't very often.

From that first day Sue and Kat just clicked, especially when they realised their senses of humour were perfectly matched. Their friendship soon left the workplace, and five years later Kat even met her husband Rob at Sue and Jeff's wedding.

Sure enough, as predicted, Sue had not even finished decanting the Welsh cakes from their paper bag onto a plate when the gannets/colleagues started arriving.

There was a cheerful, "Hi, Sue, how was the holiday? Excellent choice; makes me positively homesick," from the ever-enthusiastic and strongly Welsh-accented chief customer services operator, Trefor. He grinned his way towards the Welsh cakes, living up to every stereotype going. Trefor always complained that the versions Sue brought back were never as good as his mum's, but he would still enthusiastically eat them. After a few cheerfully sharp comments, he took the right number of them across to the other operators on shift. He knew they were tied to the phones on their desks and it was his duty as their boss to keep them provided with suitable treats.

"And don't scoff them on your way over," Sue called after him as he walked off.

"Ah, Sue, you're finally back," announced the reliably obvious and unmistakeably cold-voiced Francesca Teatherstone-Fox, their senior manager. "I don't suppose you've bothered to open your inbox yet. Head office is shrieking about the report you sent them before you left. Be in my office in ten minutes to explain your so-called findings."

Francesca gave her pronouncement as she looked down at the goodies, and trounced back to her office. Her tall, slender stature and close-cropped dark hair somehow seemed to exude cold efficiency in her tight, cropped, designer, black silk trouser suit and asymmetric white silk blouse, which was carefully chosen to be somehow stylish and yet show no personality whatsoever. Her ridiculously high-heeled shoes could be heard marching all the way back to her office.

"Typical," sighed Sue. "I don't even get a chance to say hello to my colleagues before the feared one comes down on me. I can't for a second imagine what was wrong with the report. It had all the information they wanted, and in the right format. It didn't say anything that would have surprised them." Her questions were only punctuated by the appearance of another decidedly mischievous grin. "Just because the conclusions weren't what they wanted to hear."

"Don't ask me," replied Kat. "Us underlings never get told anything. We just live to serve you haughty management types."

"Oh, sod off. Don't you put me in the same pigeonhole as 'them'. And don't eat all the Welsh cakes before the others get a chance."

She grabbed a cake to serve as her belated breakfast and went into her own office to face the onslaught that invariably lurked in her inbox whenever she'd dared to be away.

Sue sat down with her cake and her quickly made coffee from the department kitchenette and turned her computer on. She'd quickly flicked into business mode and now efficiently looked through the paper correspondence, which Kat had neatly put on her desk, while she waited for the machine to boot up. Just like the rest of the world, Sue had seen more and more communications become electronic, but there was still some paperwork to deal with. The paper pile didn't look like it contained anything scary and it could clearly wait until the electronic 'pile' was dealt with.

In years gone by, the people at the umbrella group headquarters hadn't been that bothered about Cuthbert's customer services centre, but Sue knew very well that things had changed when Francesca took up her position. They obviously had a major retail shop presence as well as an online system, where lots of money was spent on everything from the everyday shop to regular financial products. As with any such business service, backup was essential, and the service centre was where general questions got asked and any problems got dealt with.

It had always been an incredibly friendly place to work and, in the days before Francesca turned up, there had been a weekly informal competition for the most common questions from customers. Most weeks, requests for password help won, and an extra slice of the regular Friday cake was given to the person who got the most calls. Of course, Francesca put an end to this, insisting that healthy staff would be more productive than overfed staff.

At that time the bosses were considering outsourcing the customer services function to a foreign company. Sue knew very well that the customers seriously appreciated being able to talk to someone in the same country who understood the products and the kinds of problems they might have. Sue's report on the effectiveness of outsource models had shown that the company made money by attracting customers who cared about how they were treated. She had shown, with evidence, that this would be more effectively achieved in-house, which was why Francesca was so desperate to talk to her.

Francesca had been brought in to the department to make sure it was 'maximising its performance efficiency by investigating possible synergies', which everybody knew basically translated as cuts and the dreaded word 'outsourcing'. Francesca vehemently denied this but people in the real world knew that if the senior managers had their way, all their jobs would be given to seemingly cheaper people on the other side of the world. Sue was going to do everything she could to prevent this from happening. Just in her department, dozens of jobs were on the line.

When Francesca descended into her 'senior manager' role, the branch manager position Sue had held for seven years became not much more than a day-to-day operations manager. Francesca took over all the interdepartmental work and the major decision-making part of the job. The rest of the department consisted of a number of administrative staff and a large number of telephone operating staff on shifts, providing the always available and well-trained contacts the customers expected.

Sue hoped that her report would help with her mission to protect those staff, and she knew that nothing would be done with it over the two weeks she was away. The fact that Francesca was so stressed was a good sign. Once Sue's computer was booted up and she had logged in, she checked her emails. Much like the pile on her doorstep, most of it was junk, but as she had expected there was one from central management with the subject line 'Service Centre Structure'. When Sue opened it she read:

To: Susan Mead

From: Cynthia Hargreaves

cc: John Teatherstone-Fox; Francesca Teatherstone-Fox

Subject: Service Centre Structure

TEATHERSTONE-FOX GROUP – Synergy in business

Dear Ms Mead

We at the central management board would like to thank you for your extensive work preparing this report. As soon as we have come to a decision regarding this matter we will communicate this to all relevant parties.

Regards
John Teatherstone-Fox
Teatherstone-Fox Group Director

In his usual style, the director of the Teatherstone-Fox umbrella company, Francesca's father, hadn't even bothered to send the just-about-polite holding letter himself, passing that job onto his secretary. In her usual style, Cynthia Hargreaves had used Sue's least favoured way of being addressed. Sue hated being called a Ms; she frequently signed her emails as Mrs. Ms Hargreaves might like the Ms but it felt like a lazy assumption. Of course, it could have been a deliberate but cheap way of trying to wind Sue up.

Even though the email itself was short and apparently meaningless, there were two possible interpretations that Sue could see. Either John TF was being a typical senior manager and completely failing to make a decision, so he got his faithful secretary to send a nice-sounding holding email; or alternatively, and far more likely, he had made his decision long ago, didn't like the undeniable conclusion of Sue's report, and was trying to work out a spin he could use to get the answer he wanted.

Sue felt a little bit mischievous that she had made sure Francesca had seen the report just after the holiday had started, but in her defence, John TF had dictated the timing so it wasn't really her fault. Either way, she knew the meeting she was about to have with Francesca would be 'interesting'. Fifteen minutes after her 'invitation', the longest time Sue felt she could get away with.

2

If it wasn't for the completely different type of work, Jeff's life looked scarily like his wife's. He'd joined the IT department about thirteen years earlier and had similarly spent many years really getting to know the company and its IT structure. He had a strong hatred of people who just told other people what to do without being willing to get their hands dirty themselves and without really understanding how the real world worked. He dreaded to think how many times over his career he had asked himself what those managers' purpose really was. So, he made very sure he knew the whole system inside and out before he went anywhere near management. Even then, he only became the IT branch manager when his old boss, Terry, had retired six and a half years earlier.

Jeff's department was structured much like Sue's, with a more senior member of the Teatherstone-Fox Group taking senior managerial control, with Jeff as the day-to-day manager. Under him, although he really didn't like looking at it that way, were the rest of the IT team, who did the bulk of the work, keeping the online presence working smoothly and Cuthbert's actual IT infrastructure going. This included running a help service when colleagues had computer problems, which regularly featured requests for password resets. The same human frailties applied equally to Sue's external customers and Jeff's internal users.

Again, much like Sue's situation, everything in the history-laden company had changed when the take-over happened.

The early history of the company was very well known. In 1842, Cuthbert Horace Rigby, a prominent local Chartist spokesman, used his family name linked to riches from their part in the Yorkshire steel-based industrial revolution, to open a small chain of general grocery shops for the local workforce. Even though he was the second son, and wasn't going to inherit the family fortune, the name was still useful to get the loan he needed to start a grocery business.

His strong Chartist beliefs, including that every working man over twenty-one deserved a vote, led to his horror at the common living conditions and the inaccessibility of decent, reasonably priced food. He had no power to change the way his family's fortune was made, but he knew he could do something to make people's lives better. To support local farmers, he made sure that as much as possible the food was sourced locally, the farmers were paid reasonably and the customers were not overcharged. Unlike some of his competitors, he accepted the fact that this might mean that his profits, while liveable, were not excessive. His industrialist family didn't understand his beliefs but, in modern parlance, he was very successfully rebelling against their behaviour.

Cuthbert proudly opened his first shop in the building the loan had bought in the centre of a residential area. This all happened not long before photography was invented; so, as soon as possible, there was the classic proud photograph of Cuthbert in front of the first shop, with rows of good quality produce behind him.

Over many successful years Cuthbert's became a household name across the country, largely by broadening its scope, always keeping up to date but always staying true to the original morals. Its products were sourced as locally to each shop as possible, and the shops ranged from the many ubiquitous small corner shops to a few larger outlets. It managed to stay family-owned, and as younger generations came in they did things like include more upmarket products along with the decent basic food they'd started on. They also provided fairly managed financial services, loans, savings, insurance and the like. It became so entrenched in society, it even became part of the English language. From the very early days, customers would say they were 'going down Berty's' for their shopping. 'Berty to the rescue' became accepted slang for getting an emergency pint of milk from the local corner shop, which even got formally rebadged as Berty's to set it apart from the bigger supermarket and the financial end of the business.

Right from the outset, people enjoyed working for Cuthbert's. Part of original plan was to pay people decently. This was only partly altruistic; after all, happy employees did a better job and helped get more happy customers. As soon as he started making a profit he added to the staff wages by giving them a small share.

It was only when the chain started expanding to other cities, a generation or so after it was founded, that the headquarters needed to be moved to a dedicated new building. It was a fine late-Victorian building that eventually became dwarfed by the practical office blocks around it. Over time, even they got replaced by bigger and more comfortable office 'spaces', as the modern terminology put it. Despite the industrial scale of the newer buildings, they were practically and comfortably set up, with plenty of space for meetings that weren't going to disturb people working. There were plenty of improvements, like chairs that were comfortable but not too comfortable, so working was easier. A reasonable number of relaxing spaces and kitchen facilities were provided, for lunches and any caffeine needed. Of course, any special needs, like bad backs, were catered for as a matter of course, long before it became a legal necessity.

As working practices developed over the years, there was always a good balance of open working spaces where collaboration was needed, and private offices where people needed quiet. Office doors were rarely closed when Jeff started working there.

By the time Sue and Jeff came to work there, the way of working had firmly embedded itself into the building structure. Because the IT department and the service centre had to do much work together, they were sited at opposite ends of the same floor in the same building.

Of course, they were a money-making company and still had to keep up with modern ways, which was a major part of Jeff's job. Cuthbert's was one of the first to get into things like the internet purchasing world, for both groceries and financial products. They saw the customer services benefits and, of course, the profits to be made. Following their longstanding ethos and moral standards, they used service providers who invested money locally and ethically. Always, exploitation was avoided and the environment cared for, long before it became widely known as a major problem. This made them very popular. Despite what some marketing people said, people really appreciated being treated like adults and they wanted good products sold at a reasonable price. It had worked for the groceries for all those years, and the financial stuff was no different. They actually became one of the top eight financial products providers in the country.

Most of the actual financial decisions were made by the relevant providers, the experts in the financial world. Due to a peculiarity of the banking system, while the money for the groceries and other one-off payments bypassed Cuthbert's and went straight to the supplier's bank, the direct debits went through Cuthbert's accounts directly. Jeff had been a major player in the IT department, writing software to run the required websites. The IT department provided all the essential background services, like emailing details of the financial products available to existing customers, along with any offers that were being promoted and, crucially for a money-making organisation, taking the payments.

All of this had to produce a system which would never crash in the middle of a customer's visit and would be completely usable by all their potential customers. It was obvious from their overall ethos that they would follow expert advice on making their website easy to use by people with reduced eyesight, dyslexia, poor coordination or other physical problems. Of course, any website that takes people's money needs a good customer services department that has easy access to people's details. Jeff and Sue actually met at a meeting to discuss what was needed from that software.

Things continued on like this for a few years, the company ethically making a very healthy amount of money, which made Cuthbert's very attractive to people whose sole purpose was to make as much money as possible.

Suddenly it became impossible to remain a family-run business.

For generations the business had happily stayed within the Rigby family, with the forward-thinking Andrew taking over in 1972. He was the holder of the head role when computers became good enough and, much later, the web became clever enough to bring it into the business. He made the decisions that made sure the best people were brought in and given everything they needed to make the whole computer 'revolution' work for Cuthbert's.

He and his wife, Ruth, only had one daughter, Sally, who grew up to be a very intelligent woman with a very level business head. Andrew and Ruth were determined to make sure that Sally was allowed to find her own way in the world and make her own choices, but they couldn't help being very relieved when she showed great interest in Cuthbert's. As a young adult, Sally went to business school to learn about modern business practices, and then spent several years in various different businesses learning what worked and what was best left in an academic book. She also spent many years working within Cuthbert's, really getting to know how the company worked and where new ideas could be applied. She knew that the best way of finding out how most effectively to make the daily work successful, and where it might be improved, was by talking to the people who did it.

As Andrew got into his later years and was looking forward to retirement, Sally became more and more ready to take over from him. Actually, his health was starting to cause problems and retirement was fast becoming more of a necessity.

Tragically, not long before the changeover was due to happen, Sally was killed in an accident involving her small car and a large lorry. During her time working at Cuthbert's she had got to know many staff members, some of whom had become good friends, so everyone was shocked and heartbroken by her death. Her parents never really recovered. Everyone was also very worried about what this meant for their future.

Within a week of Sally's very well-attended funeral, the older members of the family were approached by people none of them had ever heard of with an offer to buy the company. They were assured that while they were being offered a very attractive deal, the ethics of the company would always be preserved. Given the urgency of the situation, the Cuthbert's lawyers did some very brief investigating into Teatherstone-Fox's history. They found that they had indeed bought out a few fairly successful businesses, which later became even more profitable, enough to allow the Teatherstone-Fox Group to purchase the next moderately successful business.

There was also a totally irrationally placed feeling that because the Teatherstone-Fox Group was also a family-owned company, which had made its very large amount of money by 'enhancing a full portfolio of already successful businesses', it would respect those agreements. So promised their affable founder, John Teatherstone-Fox. Mr Teatherstone-Fox, or John as he insisted on being called by all at the time, looked to be in his late fifties or early sixties. He'd obviously been quite fit in his youth but age and good living had helped fill out his body to plumpness, which he made friendly jokes about. He had a voice that showed working-class roots that he was keen to emphasise, showed his understanding of Cuthbert's origins.

All of the bureaucracy involved in any of the other choices, such as going public or a staff buyout, seemed impossible in the time available so the Teatherstone-Fox offer was the only viable option.

The ink was only just dry on the sales documents before it started to become obvious that they were only paying lip service to the whole old-fashioned values part of the deal. The company staff soon found out that John Teatherstone-Fox's 'affability' was just as fake as those promises.

The very well paid Teatherstone-Fox lawyer made sure that appropriate wording was used to stretch the definitions in those 'promises' as far as possible. The groceries started being made more profitably with cheaper, imported ingredients. Unsurprisingly, the prices stayed the same so the earnings went up. The customers did start noticing the difference but the convenience of the Berty's shops meant a lot, even though the unique selling point was disappearing fast.

Even the language within Cuthbert's changed. John Teatherstone-Fox's intrinsic straightforwardness was replaced with more business-speak than anyone knew existed, coming from the sharp suits that surrounded him. The Teatherstone-Fox Group was into 'modernising', 'streamlining' and 'maximising synergies' within the structure of the company. People would have found this funny if they didn't know it meant they had to start worrying about their jobs.

Of course, they made a lot of seemingly small but infuriating changes designed to stamp their identity onto the organisation. At one end of the annoyance scale were stupid things, like dictating that all internal communications, paper or electronic, had to be headed by the Teatherstone-Fox Group logo, even one-sentence emails. At the other end of the scale, the accounting department had to completely change its reporting mechanisms. They had to be able to pass the information on how much money had been spent, taken and finally made each month, back to the central Teatherstone-Fox Group bosses. This drove everybody mad, having to translate what had been a perfectly efficient accounting system into a different and very unwieldy system. It was all so some accountant somewhere could report back to the bosses on whether profits were going up or down and what was making the most or least money. This of course pointed to where corners could be cut and more money made.

Soon after the takeover, the big boss's son, Nicholas, suddenly turned up in the IT department to run it the Teatherstone-Fox Group way. Surprisingly, for an obvious money-grabber's son, he knew a reasonable amount about IT. He was a strange combination of practical IT developer who understood how that part of the world truly worked and spoilt rich kid. His language was far more down to earth than the rest of the Teatherstone-Fox Group's suits but he still made sure people knew who was in control. He clearly demonstrated his self-defined importance by declaring one of the side meeting rooms to be his private office so he never had to work as part of the general IT team. Unlike the family photos many of the team had on their desks, TF Junior's office remained stark and unadorned.

One of the first things he did was bury himself away, learning how the various IT systems fitted together. He only occasionally came out of his office to bark at one of the other staff members, demanding to know how this or that part worked. Often there were arguments about why on earth, in his opinion, stupid decisions had been made about how things were structured, even though they had always worked very efficiently.

Despite considerable technical knowledge, TF Junior, as he became quietly known in the IT department, had his own ideas about how things like IT should be run. Jeff had tried to argue hard that the IT department knew best what the real requirements were and that senior management's wishes were irrelevant if the department was going to be able to provide what would really make the place work. To get the best job done they had to talk to the people who actually used the system and ask them what they needed, rather than dictating what they'd get, like it or not.

Of course, the root of the problem, not that TF Junior realised there was one, was the very definition of 'need'. The TF clan defined it as anything that would make them money. The original Cuthbert's staff stuck to the fast disappearing idea of 'what's best for the customer'. The two ideas should have ended up with the same bottom line but the Teatherstone-Fox Group wasn't interested in the middle step.

Unfortunately, TF Junior, who clearly represented his father, had the final say and announced that he wanted the whole IT system to be rebuilt to use a particular software package that some slick salesmen had convinced them would do a better job than the package that had been previously used. Of course, the salesmen knew better than to go straight to the IT professionals because they would see through the obvious holes.

*

When Jeff logged on, the size of his inbox mirrored Sue's, largely filled with junk. Jeff grabbed the holiday goodies and headed off to the monthly team meeting to discuss any developments in the IT department.

Luckily for Jeff's team, TF Junior wasn't there that day, so his meeting went as it should. A good meeting should always have a mutually decided objective, or at least a clear series of discussion points. The personalities involved should include a good leader to make sure the discussions stay reasonably within the agreed limits. They have to make sure that no one person, including themselves, dominates the discussion, preventing other people from getting across what might be valid points. Everyone should listen to everyone else and respect their opinions, even if they don't agree with them. Without TF Junior's overbearing personality, actual work could get done. Jeff made sure that only people who really had to be disturbed from their work were at the meeting. He intended it to be as short as possible, just long enough to get an update on the progress of the different work areas while he'd been away, and progress on any of the major bits of work.

As soon as he got to the meeting room the mirroring of Sue's day was complete.

"Welsh cakes, again!"

*

9.21am

Their general situations were very similar but Sue's meeting could not have been more different.

Sue walked in to Francesca's office with a printout of the report ready to refer to and was greeted by her very impatient boss with one of her precious espressos in one of her precious fine china cups. It was a regular joke between Sue and Kat that the coffee would taste just the same from the cheap range that Cuthbert's homeware department sold, but Francesca insisted on drinking her own blend from expensive cups. She always washed them herself and kept them locked away when she wasn't there.

"What do you mean by submitting that pile of nonsense just as you gallivant off on your jollies?" Francesca Teatherstone-Fox snapped before Sue had even shut the office door.

"Everything in that report is well evidenced and logically presented" Sue calmly answered, resolutely refusing from the start to get riled up. She started to sit down in one of

Francesca's seriously stylish and incredibly uncomfortable chairs as she tried to finish her first sentence.

When Francesca descended on the department, the previous manager's cheerful cartoon posters, poking gentle fun at a typical workplace, and her comfortable armchairs were summarily replaced. The whole office had been re-styled by the London-based company Francesca brought in on her arrival. Cartoons that would make people smile were replaced by very carefully and impersonally chosen 'modern art' that at best was considered bland. The less diplomatic staff called them ugly. The welcoming comfort was replaced by seating which made it very clear that the woman behind the 'stylish' desk was in charge.

This of course fitted perfectly with Francesca's overall look. While everyone else in the department dressed comfortably enough to get the job done, Francesca obviously believed that anyone successful in business had to look the part at all times. Sue and the rest of management normally wore smart suits, with the jackets taken off as soon as they got into work. Francesca always wore the latest designer trouser suits and white blouses, with her jacket on at all times. To most people they all looked the same: black suit, white blouse and very high heels.

"Well, I don't recognise any of the points you made," Francesca interrupted, "and the conclusions could only have come from your imagination. The examples you used were irrelevant and bore no relation to our situation."

"Actually," Sue calmly but strongly stated as soon as Francesca stopped to take a breath, "the other organisations are incredibly similar to ours, as I explained in Section 2, and the research clearly shows that outsourcing, especially offshoring, of customer services could produce a highly detrimental effect on public opinion, and consequently company turnover, and eventually the customers would go elsewhe…"

"The more highly respected evidence we have seen," Francesca retorted in the most superior-sounding voice she could muster, "clearly shows that full briefing of an external service centre will facilitate a perfectly adequate functionality, especially when it is supported by an efficient IT infrastructure."

Sue was always amazed at how wonderfully stereotypical Francesca could be, spouting the classic 'management speak' and sounding like a character from a certain 1990s satirical newsroom sitcom. Before they'd met, Sue hadn't believed that someone with such a one-dimensional character could actually exist, but so far she had completely failed to find any sign of any other dimensions. She refused to be drawn by the very obvious dig at her husband's IT department.

"I would be very interested in seeing that evidence because everything I saw showed that such a system would only work if the investment put into it was greater than the savings that would be made. Besides which, I wouldn't want to work anywhere that settled on being 'adequate' when our customer base has come to expect an exceptional service that we are proud…"

"I've never seen any evidence of your so-called pride. The 'beloved' customers don't give a flying hoot about who they talk to as long as they get an answer."

This was starting to make Sue's grip on her own calmness even harder to maintain. Doing her best, while increasing the firmness in her voice, she replied, "Are you willing to pay out the significant costs of training the outsource staff to the level of knowledge our staff have? Are you willing to pay out more for ongoing training if you fail to find a company that avoids regular staff turnover? Will you make sure the requirements are defined well enough and the payment terms aimed at maintaining the levels of customer satisfaction we know we provide? Will the levels of communication be maintained, to ensure the management, the operating staff and the infrastructure providers all work together?"

"Thank you, Ms Mead, for asking all of the questions our corporate operatives are quite capable of recognising as good questions. I can assure you that all of the important issues will be addressed."

Sue was fairly sure there was a derisory edge to the way Francesca said 'good' and 'important' but knew she was in too much danger of losing her composure, so she made herself calm down.

And so it continued for another half an hour, going round and round, with Francesca getting more and more irate and rarely letting Sue finish her arguments. Sue resolutely refused to rise, or in her view sink, to the same level. She very carefully started talking only when Francesca paused to draw breath, which she seemed to do surprisingly rarely. It was very obvious that Sue's calmness was a major part of Francesca's irritation. Sue knew very well that the fastest way to wind up someone who was desperate for a fight was to refuse to fight back.

Francesca was many things but she was not an idiot; she knew exactly what Sue was trying to do. Every now and then Francesca would take a deep breath, close her eyes for a moment, force herself to calm down and start going through Sue's arguments rationally. But ridiculously quickly, that very rationality started getting her back up again and she would come dangerously close to losing her temper.

"Have you quite finished interrupting me?" Francesca demanded. "You clearly made up your mind without any credible evidence and you obviously don't care about anyone else's opinion but your own!" Sue couldn't help smiling at the blatant hypocrisy.

Determined to be the one who got to decide when the conversation ended, and thinking she was in control, Francesca decided to change tack and go for the just as obviously fake and chummy 'we're all in this together' style.

"Look, Sue, clearly this conversation is going nowhere. We both need to step away, clear our heads and get a more rational view. Everybody wants what's best, so let's reconvene at a later date. Perhaps with my father here. I'll arrange it and get back to you with the date."

Sue walked back to her office amused by the thought that the entire conversation could have been over in thirty seconds rather than thirty minutes if they had both said what they really meant.

What was even more amusing from Sue's point of view was the pointlessness of the whole thing. The Teatherstone-Fox Group were the bosses. They had the power to simply decide that the customer services department was going to be outsourced. She knew very well that they had only told her to write the report assuming she would be a good little employee and say what they wanted to hear. If she had followed the corporate line, that whole meeting wouldn't have been needed at all. The only problem was, she enjoyed telling the truth far too much when it annoyed annoying people. As she went back to her office she wondered where that mischievous streak came from.

3

August

Jennifer pulled her Alfa Romeo 8C convertible up to the pavement in a smart side road of the Bern financial district, in front of the small but exclusive Swiss bank. As her husband got out of the passenger seat she let her door be opened by the waiting valet.

"Good morning, Mrs Page. It's a pleasure to see you again," said young Tobias in impeccable English but with his natural Germanic accent.

"Thank you. It's just a shame to have to go inside on such a beautiful day."

"Indeed."

The weather was indeed lovely on this August day, not oppressively hot and beautifully sunny, just as this particular pair of customers liked it. As far as they were concerned it was one of the major attractions to that part of the world. The local summers were never too hot and the Swiss mountains always provided un-ignorable beauty.

While Tobias took Jennifer's place in the driver's seat to take the car to the valet parking, her husband walked around to join her. She took his arm, gave it a fond and gentle squeeze, and they walked towards the bank.

Their accents may have been British but Jennifer and Mark were clearly a couple who embraced classic Italian style. The bright red Italian sports car was perfectly complemented by its owners. They gently strolled towards the entrance with an air so confident that it showed no air at all. There was no brashness or ostentation – they just wore the Armani and Valentino, augmented with only a few necessary designer accessories, with natural comfort and relaxed Italian style.

As they approached the bank's door it automatically opened, and Mark paused to let his wife go in first.

They entered the stylish but understated lobby. The pale grey marble walls could have made it look cold and sterile but the beautiful walnut-veneered desks at which various staff members sat warmed the place. Herr Gyger came over with his usual efficiency. His dark suit and pale burgundy tie, together with neatly folded matching handkerchief in the breast pocket, and his neatly combed salt and pepper hair, complemented the surroundings perfectly.

"Mr and Mrs Page, it is always a pleasure to see you. I hope you are well. Mrs Page, you are as beautiful as ever," he said in his mildly accented but perfect English, with a smile and a slight bow. He had a well-practised manner that might have seemed cheesy on many other men but on him came across as a thoroughly believable and understated charm.

"And you are as charming as ever," Jennifer said, holding out her hand to shake his in her regular firm but not overly aggressive way.

"Tell me," said Mark, shaking the bank manager's hand and wryly smiling, "are you even more friendly with your customers who have more money than us?"

"I am equally friendly with all our customers," he said with a matching smile.

"Even the ones with less money?"

"With all our customers, no matter what their circumstances!" he said in mock horror but with a sly smile. "We just have a minimum deposit required to become a customer."

By this point in the conversation he had effortlessly guided Jennifer and Mark towards his office, and he graciously allowed them to enter first. They sat down on the dark leather sofa he offered them and he sat opposite in the matching leather armchair. His secretary followed them in with their favourite espressos.

Everything was done as effortlessly as it should be. Neither of the two customers could help privately enjoying the fact that with their money they could come to the bank dressed casually, without the need for classically British conservatism. The strict dark woollen suits expected in London would have been unbearably hot here. With money came comfort.

The meeting went along at an unhurried yet businesslike pace. Jennifer and Mark checked that their regular and reasonably sizeable deposits were being used in sensible but agreeable investments. It was essential to Jennifer and Mark that their money was used profitably but not in any way that would cause harm to the things they cared about. It probably meant they made less money than they could have done but they were comfortable and the environment was protected. More importantly to them, no employees in any company they invested money in were exploited. When they were assured that their values were being adhered to they got to the real reason for their visit.

"Between us, our trust funds are due to mature over the next few years so we wanted to start exploring our options to maintain a, shall we say, comfortable income into the future," said Mark.

"May one ask how big your endowments will be?" enquired Herr Gyger.

"Of course, that's your job," said Jennifer. "They are due to be ten times as much as we've received so far."

"And what are your plans for that money?"

"Our requirements are relatively modest," Mark said. "We intend to purchase some property and then ensure we have a good income for as long as needed."

Herr Gyger knew what 'as long as needed' really meant, so neither customer felt the need to be tactlessly frank.

The rest of the conversation followed along those lines, covering possible investments that would meet Jennifer and Mark's financial needs while sticking within their moral requirements. Once they were done, Herr Gyger led them into a back room, to a brass-decorated elevator and then down to the safety deposit box vault. He and the security attendant posted at a desk just outside used their security keys to open the gate covering the open vault door. They knew that Herr Gyger respected the privacy of the other customers who owned the several hundred or so locked boxes in the vault, just as much as he respected theirs. They watched him use his key again to release their one comparatively small box from its cabinet. The regular routine was insisted on by the bank, to prove that they had the correct box. After they were left alone in a quiet private room, where they used their own key to open the box, they added an envelope to the others already there. Then the entire process was repeated in reverse to demonstrate that the same box was properly secured.

It was just about lunchtime when Jennifer and Mark finished at the bank so they went straight for a light lunch at a nearby café full of local business people grabbing quick bites. Jennifer and Mark were able to take a little more time over their bratwurst and balsamic mustard crunchy rolls, but then, their time was their own. When they were done they drove to the nearby Laténium Celtic archaeological museum to indulge in a particular passion.

They had deliberately timed their visit to coincide with a new exhibition of stunning art and jewellery in the Le Tène mid-continental Celtic style. Some histories painted them as little more than savages but the fineries and traded goods showed much greater depth. Jennifer strongly felt that even though they came from violent times, and the number of ornately decorated weaponry showed their violent side, no civilisation that survived for over 400 years and that made such beautiful torques, armlets and intricately woven patterns could be all bad.

It seemed to Jennifer that it was only when some of the Romans, and probably some others, came in, forced their will on the world and brutally got rid of anyone who disagreed with them, that saw the end to that civilisation. Something truly rankled her about that.

*

Afterwards, the Pages drove to the central but elegant hotel they were spending the night in. It wasn't the most expensive hotel in town but was only one step down on the price scale; they had found somewhere that mixed the desired level of luxury with a more relaxed atmosphere. This was far more their style. The décor was modern without being cold, and the staff were efficient and polite without being standoffish.

They showered in their suite and changed into equally elegant evening outfits. They very much enjoyed dressing up for their evening meal but never in a way that took effort to wear. Jennifer's slim figure slid perfectly into the dark green D&G lace dress. Mark had an untucked and untied way of wearing his D&G dinner suit that looked and felt easy, and to Jennifer's eyes was incredibly sexy. As she got dressed his eyes made it very obvious that he also appreciated how she looked in her dress.

In the same way as the rest of the hotel, the semi-informal style of the brasserie had everything needed to make it good enough to class it as high dining. It was world-renowned for a wonderful mixture of locally inspired dishes and food with flavours from around the world. Always, the main ingredients were as local and seasonal as possible, a philosophy Mark and Jennifer approved of, but the chef was not afraid to use exotic flavours to put his own stamp on some of the dishes.

"*Guten abend, Herr und Frau Page.* Please come this way," the maître d' said as soon as they walked in the door, and he led them straight to their two-person table in one of the slightly quieter corners of the room. There were a few other diners already enjoying their meals but the room was so well laid out that they could quite easily ignore each other if they so wished. But they had all been there the previous night and were friendly enough for a nod of recognition or a quiet '*guten abend*' as they passed.

As they reached their table the same waitress as last night, Lisle, was waiting for them and was introduced by the maître d', who then pulled Jennifer's chair back. In the same smooth movement Jennifer sat in the offered chair and took a menu from Lisle. Mark sat in the other chair and opened his menu.

"What is particularly good tonight?" Jennifer asked as she looked over the choices.

"As I remember, you like our local food more than the more exotic, so may I recommend the calf's head with mustard vinaigrette, or the Zurich-style rose veal."

"Does Zurich count as local?" Mark asked with his usual half smile.

"Don't be so pedantic," Jennifer responded. "I'll have the regional cold meats and cheese starter, please, followed by the calf's head."

"And I'll have the same starter, and the veal sounds lovely." Mark was happy to compromise his usual wish for more traditional food with the more humanely raised rose veal.

"And may I suggest a lovely vintage Altenbourg Gewurztraminer to accompany both?" the sommelier said as he silently appeared alongside Lisle. The waiting staff had that great skill of not being obtrusive when they weren't needed but always there when they were.

The quality and the enjoyment of the meal did not surprise them. The only thing they did not understand was why the chef had not yet been given a Michelin star. It may have been true that the regional meats and cheeses were simply expertly sourced high-quality produce presented with great respect, but somehow when it came to the table it was raised to a different level. Once upon a time the calf's head would have been a pauper's dish, making best use of every morsel of precious meat. Now, like so many basic meats, it had been taken and made sophisticated for the well-to-do. Whilst it was definitely added to here, it was never played with unnecessarily.

The long, slow-simmered calf's head was turned into a densely packed terrine, layered with local heritage potatoes and herbs and served with a cake of the same potatoes. The Zurich veal was prepared with locally grown cremini mushrooms and a potato and sweet potato rösti. The relaxed feeling of the brasserie meant that Mark and Jennifer had no compunction about reaching across and trying each other's food and laughing over their enjoyment of what had once been pauper's food in a grand hotel.

Dessert was a selection of typical Bernese patisserie followed by an Armagnac each. They then went back to their suite and got an early night. As they lay there, gently nuzzling between fine Indian cotton bedsheets, Mark squeezed his wife even closer and softly whispered:

"I know I'm supposed to say that cuddling you is wonderful in any bed, but it does feel extra special here."

"I know exactly what you mean," Jennifer agreed with a soft smile, and snuggled into him even further.

Fairly early the next morning, after a beautiful eggs Benedict served in the suite, they set off and took a gentle drive through the Alps back to their apartment in Milan.

They could have taken the faster route but they deliberately chose slightly slower, even more scenic roads and savoured the great joy of driving an open-topped car through some of the most stunning mountain scenery in the world. The main road took them due south from Bern and then they turned off towards Interlaken to enjoy the lake views. Rather than going into the touristy town centre, they stopped by a particularly beautiful spot, and there were many to choose from, and lunched on the lovely picnic hamper the hotel had provided for them.

Once the car engine was turned off they sat for a moment revelling in the pure air, hearing nothing but a nearby stream trickling over mountain rocks. They looked at each other and smiled. They didn't have to say anything because they both knew just how lucky they were. For what felt like the billionth time, Jennifer felt glad she had never got used to this scenery to the point of not appreciating it anymore.

Later that afternoon they got back to Milan. They were just early enough to miss the afternoon rush hour but knew very well that it didn't really matter when it came to Italian city drivers. Jennifer had quickly learned that everyone had to drive with a confident aggression in order to get anywhere, so in reasonably quick time they entered the underground parking lot beneath their apartment block. Some years before, they had carefully chosen this three-bedroom apartment as an occasional home on a central side street, which was comfortable and stylish enough for them, and close but not too close to the centre of the city. They could easily get to their favourite restaurants and the vibrant social life but they weren't on top of the many tourists. Whilst they enjoyed the trappings of finer cuisine, they also thoroughly enjoyed the wonderful Italian food that could be found in any local restaurant just off the tourist trails.

Jennifer swept her card across the sensor at the barrier and the disembodied voice of the receptionist came through the adjacent speaker:

"Buona sera, Seniora Page."

"Buona sera, Stephano," she said as she smiled at the CCTV camera above the barrier.

At the same time the barrier to the underground car park opened and Jennifer drove the Alfa out of the afternoon sunshine. Another swipe of their key card made sure the elevator from the car park took them straight up to their apartment level. Jennifer went straight to the kitchen to get the espresso maker ready for their favourite blend. The kitchen may have been stylishly modern but no Italian kitchen would be without a proper espresso maker. At the same time, Mark took the travel bags into the main bedroom. Leaving them by the wardrobe, he walked into the kitchen where Jennifer was reaching into the cupboard for the tiny coffee cups and put his arms around her.

"Do we really need coffee right now? I think we should lie down after such a long journey," he said, while his hands made it very clear that rest was the last thing on his mind. Jennifer smiled and gently slapped one of his wandering hands.

"We're having dinner with Caterina and Carlo this evening, remember?" she said as she turned around, putting her arms over his shoulders.

"Yes, but we don't have to be there for hours," he answered as he gently stroked her face and tenderly pulled her chin up so their lips met. Jennifer very happily responded and turned the hob off under the espresso maker. They both smiled as they went into the bedroom.

4

July

"Happy anniversary, you great old nerd!" Rob proclaimed with a grin as Jeff opened the front door to Rob and Kat and Rob handed over one of several bottles of real ale.

"How many times do I have to tell you?" Jeff answered as he appreciatively looked over the beer. "I am a geek, not a nerd – they're into *Star Trek*, not IT."

"Yeah, but you're into that too."

"Yeah, all right, I'll give you that," Jeff answered with a shrug and a sly grin. "But only if you admit you're as bad as me, you great hypocrite," he pointedly replied on the way to the pre-made table in their dining room. "Anyway, young people have anniversaries too aand clearly forty-two is the new thirty-two, so less of the 'old' if you don't mind. Anyway, how about you, you equally 'old' git? How is the world of private IT forensics going? Found anything interesting recently?"

Rob and Jeff had known each other for years and had formed what felt like a lifelong friendship based on a common love of all things IT. Rob had become a computer fraud policeman but had then left the force and set himself up as a quite successful private investigator doing the same sort of work.

Oddly, their meeting had nothing to do with IT. One Friday night about fifteen and a half years earlier, they had both had long weeks at work and felt an overpowering need for a good beer before going home, poured well and not out of a bottle. Jeff, his boss Terry and a few other real ale-loving members of the IT department were of the same mind so the small group arrived at about 6.30pm. The rest of the group really did only want a single pint each but, being younger, Jeff still had the wish for another, so he found himself at the bar alone.

The pub being a very welcoming place, where people felt comfortable on their own, Rob had had no issue with turning up alone at about 7.30pm; it had been a very long day. So, the young police officer and the IT developer both happened to be next to each other at the same bar, in the same local real ale pub. Jeff was the first to get served and he treated himself to his favourite. Rob overheard the request and decided he'd try one as it was new to him. With his policeman's eye he also noticed that the tired-looking drinker beside him had put a laptop-carrying backpack on the floor that looked almost identical to the one he had still over his shoulder.

"I'll try the same as this gentleman," Rob told the barman when he switched his attention to the new customer.

When the pint was poured and tasted, Rob realised it had been a good choice and raised his glass in a toast of thanks to the like-minded stranger. The conversation started from there, and over fifteen years later they were still appreciating good beer together.

Jeff grabbed the handily placed bottle opener/corkscrew off the dining table and opened the gratefully received gifts, and they toasted Rob's silent acceptance that he was just as much of a computer lover.

"Shall we pander to the classic stereotypes and finish making dinner while the men talk rubbish?" Sue's colleague and, more importantly, best friend Kat asked as she brought her contribution of a bottle of red wine into the kitchen that led to the dining room. "Happy Anniversary," she added as she hugged and kissed her friend.

"Thank you, sweetheart," Sue replied as she poured a glass from the bottle she'd already opened and handed it over almost automatically. "I did think about sticking to feminist principles and joining in with them for about 5 milliseconds before I remembered how boring they can get, so went back to the cooking. Besides which, I want to stay out of any age-related conversations. Rob might remember I'm a year older than Jeff."

"I know exactly what you mean. And you're right about talking rubbish. They actually used the words 'IT' and 'interesting' in the same sentence. I'd rather concentrate on the important stuff. What is for dinner?"

Sue replied, "I've gone for the classic but unbeatable Italian."

"What about your beloved Welsh?"

"We've just had a visit, eating loads of Welsh food, and what can I say, I fancied a change. We're having antipasti... sorry, a starter," Sue said when she noticed Kat's puzzled face, "of fresh artichoke heart salad, a first course of seafood linguini; the main course will be pork in a stunning balsamic vinegar reduction, and a limoncello panna cotta for desert."

"Surely you should say that sounding like an Italian waiter if you're going to do it properly," Rob jokingly called through from the dining room, interrupting the ongoing computer talk.

"*Per antipasti, é insalata di* something – that means, fresh artichoke," Sue pronounced in a totally over the top, enthusiastically loud Italian *mamma* style, even though she didn't seem to have all the right words. "*Il primi piati é linguini con fruiti di mare. Secondi é porc con salsa di aceto balsamico e per la dolce é pane cotte di limoncello.*"

"Where did you learn to speak Italian so well?" Kat asked.

"Oh, I just pick bits up from watching too many Italian cookery programmes," Sue answered, a little embarrassed. "Anyway, everything's ready. Let's get eating," she announced as she grabbed the starter and brought it through to the table. "And my only condition for producing this glorious food is that there will be no work talk over dinner."

The boys did as they were told over dinner, and the meal carried on resembling a great Italian one: there was great food, a lot of wine, great laughter and conversation, and everyone seriously enjoyed the company. Sue had carefully planned the meal so that most of it could be easily finished and brought to the table and she didn't have to spend too much time away from the enjoyment. Even when she had to see to the food in the kitchen she was still close enough to keep checking that her work-talk moratorium was observed.

At the end of the meal they all took their wines and beers into the living room, leaving the kitchen looking like a dirty dishes bomb had gone off in it. Rob made a token, and blatantly insincere, move towards tidying, only to get firmly told that the dishes were for tomorrow.

"And now for tonight's main attraction!" Jeff announced as they all got comfortable in the living room.

"What are you on ab..." started Sue, a little uncomfortably, as things suddenly didn't quite look as she'd expected.

"As well you might ask, pretty lady," Jeff firmly interrupted, standing up with his wine glass raised as though for a toast. "As it is our tenth anniversary I have a little present for my darling wife."

"But we agreed to watch the money..."

"Panic ye not. Rob kindly helped me put together something I know you will enjoy. As we got married on a bit of a shoestring and the photos and video were done by our friends, we never got around to making a pretty compilation. So, I gave Rob all of the stuff we did have and he used that IT skill of his that you are so derisory about to make the following video. Mr Geek, if you would be so kind."

"It would be my pleasure, Mr Geek," Rob answered with a smile as he turned on the telly and started the pre-loaded DVD.

What followed was a very skilfully stitched-together combination of scanned photos, amateur video and added soundtrack from Sue and Jeff's wedding. It started predictably enough with a photo another friend had taken of Jeff and Rob, his best man, arm in arm with cans of beer in their hands, grinning cheerfully. Clearly this was taken early in the day because they only had their trousers on, with their shirts and waistcoats hanging off their shoulders. Then it smoothly transitioned to the video Kat, as Sue's bridesmaid, had taken of Sue putting the finishing touches to her bridal outfit. The fact that they were on a budget did not mean that they skimped on style. Kat was a very skilful amateur seamstress and had made Sue's simple yet elegant dress. Conveniently, a dropped back and A-line skirt looked great and used less fabric. She had also made her own complementary outfit and had used the same fabric to make the boys' waistcoats, which they had only been handed the night before.

Another friend had taken charge of the video while Sue and Jeff stood in the registry office reciting their vows. They wrote slightly longer than the basic vows for each other; nothing very elaborate but they wanted something better than the legal minimum. When they were declared legally married, they looked at each other as loving partners. Jeff stepped closer, stroked Sue's cheek gently, and equally gently lifted her chin up for a beautifully romantic kiss. Their small group of friends clapped, including the overly miked friend behind the camera.

The reception photos and video were packed full of friends having a great time. They'd booked the upstairs function room in a local pub for the meal and then finished the evening off with more drinking downstairs.

"Remind me," Jeff questioned Rob, "exactly what part of the evening was it when you and Kat disappeared?"

"It was love at first sight," Kat responded, gazing sloppily at her husband.

"Love?" Sue interjected.

"We may have only just met but we instantly knew we were kindred spirits," Kat responded wistfully.

"Don't give me that! You were drunk and randy, down to an entirely different kind of spirit."

They all carried on laughing and watching the show.

The obvious people missing were Jeff's and Sue's parents. Both Rob and Kat had learned very early on not to bring the subject up. Actually, Jeff always said his childhood story was a fairly boring one. His closest friends, i.e. Sue, Rob and Kat, knew that after a massive drug problem with his parents, and in the absence of any other family, the younger kids were put into care. Early on, he showed himself to be an intelligent kid and he worked hard at breaking away from the life he could have been stuck with. His early interest in computers and a strong sense of determination meant that he found his own way into the IT world. He never wanted to have anything to do with the early part of his life and never really talked about it.

Sue's life had been just as changeable. She'd never said much about her early life but one drunken girlie night about six years ago she'd unexpectedly poured her heart out to Kat. She'd had quite a normal upbringing in eastern Wales with two loving parents. They had been a bit wild in the years before Sue was born; they had spent some time breaking some of what they felt were unnecessary rules, but always made sure nobody else got hurt. They had tried their best to make sure other people's lives were better, by their own definitions. They had been worried about environmentalism and the effects of big business years before that was common.

The presence of a child brought them more into a settled, even 'standard', style of life but they still brought Sue up with a strong sense of what was right and wrong and a strong sense of concern about what was going on in the world. A natural sense of justice was always important to them.

Then one day when she was at university, studying psychology, she got the worst phone call of her life. One of her parents' neighbours rang her mobile and told her there had been a terrible car crash. Her dad had been driving back from the shops when a lorry driver who was not paying enough attention at a roundabout drove straight into his car. He was pushed sideways into a nearby brick wall and instantly crushed to death.

Sue's mum went into a dreadful state of denial and more or less lost her mind there and then. Because there was no other family Sue had to drop out of university and take care of everything, which, to make things worse, involved putting her mum in a nearby adult care home. The details were a bit sketchy, even when alcohol was helping loosen her tongue, and Sue found talking about it all difficult. So, Kat understood that whenever Sue and Jeff disappeared off to Wales, they were actually going to see Sue's mum in the very nice care home they had found for her. She also knew that Sue found the visits really difficult and didn't want to talk about them.

Both Sue and Jeff were who they were and never felt the need to explain themselves, so their wedding was full of friends and fun and nobody questioned the absence of parents.

*

"*Ciao, cari. Come stai?*" Caterina enthusiastically welcomed her dear friends and asked how they were as she opened her door.

"*Felice anniversario*." Mark wished both Caterina and her husband Stephano a happy anniversary as he and Jennifer entered the neighbouring, very stylish apartment. "We're fine, thank you. How are you two?" His Italian was pretty good but still wasn't natural. Their friends knew that both Mark and Jennifer had spent the last six or so years learning and immersing themselves in Italian, but they still felt more relaxed speaking English. Embarrassingly, Caterina and Stephano's English, which they had started learning as children, was notably better, even with their strong accents. They even managed to avoid ending all of their words with a vowel sound as a lot of Italians had grown up doing.

"*Grazie, cara*. We are both fine," Caterina said as she accepted the very nice Swiss pastries from Jennifer and they exchanged traditional double-cheek kisses.

Jennifer and Mark had met their neighbours, soon after they started renting their Milan-based holiday home, during a chance meeting in the shared lift when they were laden down with Armani bags. A very honest conversation started about the good and bad aspects of that season's collection and it instantly became obvious that they were going to get on very well. The conversation about high fashion was also mildly affected by Caterina and Stephano's full padded Lycra cycling outfits in matching Italian flag colours. Over the years, cycling had become a regular source of conversation between the two couples, although Jennifer and Mark had never reached Caterina and Stephano's level of skill. Italian hills were beautiful but very hard work, and the English couple never kept up.

One of Mark and Jennifer's reasons for choosing their holiday home in Milan was the yearly visit by the *Giro d'Italia*. They loved their cycling, and the proximity to such stunning countryside to cycle around in was another major draw. As soon as it became obvious that they had a lot in common, Caterina had invited them over for dinner that evening in a classic Italian welcoming style. The invitations and shared loves carried on whenever they were all in town.

For many generations Caterina's family had owned a successful vineyard and its associated grand house nearby, north of Milan, deep in the more mountainous part of the Italian Lombardia wine-producing region. Jennifer knew that bringing another bottle of wine wouldn't have been appropriate but she found it impossible to turn up empty-handed. Caterina and Stephano were more than happy when Jennifer arrived with a beautiful selection of artisan Swiss pastries they had picked up in Bern before they left.

"When's the family celebration?" Jennifer asked.

"We are going to the vineyard tomorrow and both entire families are having a banquet in the evening," Stephano answered as he poured and served prosecco as an aperitif. "It will be a classic Italian affair: a lot of food, wine and noise. Which is why we are so glad you two were able to be here for a quiet anniversary celebration. There will still be good food and wine but it will be a far more intimate evening. How are your works?" Stephano asked both of his friends.

"I'm thinking of branching out from just selling antique homewares to some artisan modern jewellery," answered Jennifer.

She had occasionally talked about her small antiques trading company. Her friends knew that both her and Mark's families had successful businesses that meant they didn't need to work so hard, but not using their brains was unthinkable to them. That was probably why Jennifer got on so well with Caterina. They both knew how to enjoy their money, but the thought of doing nothing else was anathema to both of them. Most of Jennifer's work was hidden from the retail consumer because she sold mainly within the trade. However, she and Caterina had spent considerable time in local antiques shops looking for possible sources.

"Modern jewellery is a bit of a change. Are you getting bored?" Caterina asked.

"Not at all. The antiques business is still my passion but there are so many interesting jewellers around now I'd like to support them. And their work is so beautiful, especially some work I've seen inspired by ancient Celtic designs. This could fast become an extra passion."

They never really talked about Mark's numerous IT-related interests. He had a strong wish to avoid talking work when he was on holiday so the subject rarely came up.

Jennifer and Mark didn't bother asking what was for dinner; they knew their friends well enough to know that whatever they'd cooked would be delicious and there would be none left at the end. The dinner consisted of the freshest vegetables and finest local beef, and the conversation varied between politics, fashion, the *Giro d'Italia* and the plentiful gossip from Caterina and Stephano's enormous families.

Like all Italian meals, the food, wine and conversation all went together seamlessly and all were very much enjoyed.

*

Stephano poured the vintage Italian brandy for the traditional after-dinner *digestivi* soon after the last morsel of delicious tiramisu was finished. They took their drinks into the comfortable but modern lounge. All of the many dishes used to prepare and enjoy the meal were left for Signora Lupo, who would come by the next morning to clean up. Even though they could afford not to, Caterina and Stephano loved cooking, but the one thing they really appreciated their money for was the ability to pay someone else to clean up afterwards.

"How are things at the vineyard?" Mark asked. "Are you implementing that new IT system you were talking about?"

"Oh, Mark," Jennifer admonished with the tone that a disapproving mother might use, "I love you for trying to avoid the IT talk but I knew it wouldn't last."

"Don't worry, darling, I was just asking about the general health of their inheritance, and hence our future enjoyment of their food," Mark responded with the tone of a scolded child and a slight smile.

"It is OK," Stephano added. "I know my friends very well and I promise that any help Mark has given me in the past with IT will remain out of the social arena."

With that assurance, the conversation carried on about Caterina and Stephano's plans for the vineyard – maintaining its organic roots while modernising where possible. It wasn't easy but they did manage to stay within Jennifer's boundaries, particularly helped by more gossip about the two seemingly infinite families.

Caterina's youngest brother and his pregnant wife were arguing over names for their soon-to-be firstborn. They were desperately trying to be diplomatic in the way they wanted to avoid following the classic Italian tradition of using their parents' names, which sounded old-fashioned to them. Her older brother's fifteen-year-old daughter had just split up with her boyfriend and was heartbroken. She was clearly annoyed by still being classed as one of the kids, even though she regarded herself a grown-up now. Surely having been in love counted for something, she'd declared. Stephano's youngest brother had just started up his own car repair business and was doing it all wrong, according to their father. Much amusement was shared between the four of them about the similarities of families all over the world.

5

"*Un cafè et un macchiato caldo, per favore*. It was fun but I'm still not buying anything," Jennifer said, first to the waiter and then to Caterina, at the coffee shop near the Milan fashion show venue they had just been to. Jennifer was no longer a complete tourist but still enough of a Brit to sometimes want a dash of steamed milk in her espresso, while Caterina of course had the real deal.

Of course, most of the seats in the shows they saw were taken up by the fashion press but they were able to secure the exclusive private seats.

"I know you love your Armani, and the new starters were very exciting," replied Caterina, wearing an eclectic mix of fun designer wear; being tall and slender she easily wore the wonderful multicoloured knitwear open jacket with patchwork blouse and denim miniskirt. She had the kind of face which, entirely naturally, hid her forty-something age and meant she could wear whatever a twenty-year-old wore.

"A bit too avant-garde for my taste. Don't get me wrong, I like good design and beautifully made clothes, but

I'm more your classic style person," Jennifer defended her stance, wearing her full Giorgio Armani outfit: a beautiful long, flowing, dark blue silk-print poncho over a classic paler blue knee-length cotton and crepe dress, together with height-enhancing three-inch heeled shoes. Her practical nature also showed in the simple short-handled red leather handbag, which, of course, was also from Armani. She knew she looked damn fine for a forty-something woman but felt her age enough to stick to timeless classics.

"And don't forget all those clothes look great on women who are a lot taller than me. I only get away with it wearing heels," Jennifer added with a wry smile.

"I do not know," Caterina continued, sipping the coffee that had just arrived, "some of those short skirts and leather jackets would suit you. And some of those Armani ballgowns were so beautiful."

"If you're going to the Oscars. My movie career isn't going that well. How about yours?"

Caterina laughed. "What did you think of the leatherware this morning? Do you see yourself as a bit of a rock chick?"

The conversation went on discussing the ins and outs of the fashion industry and the boutique jewellery business until both of them had finished their coffees. They then took up their bags, kissed each other on each cheek and said their goodbyes. Caterina left for her car and a visit to her family's estate, and Jennifer for the walk home.

There was little Jennifer liked more than a walk through the streets of Milan. The area around the official fashion show venue was packed with all the extras that went with the event. It was hard to tell who were the customers, the journalists, the designers or the supermodels. They all looked great; the only thing that set apart the owners and designers of whichever collection was about to show was the increase in their franticness and apparent stress levels.

Jennifer enjoyed watching this for a few minutes, glad not to be a part of it, but then she decided to break away and start for home through some of the quieter streets. They'd been coming here for long enough for Jennifer to know her route very well, and she headed straight for a little street that housed one of their favourite restaurants.

Carlo's was just far enough away from the main hustle and bustle to avoid being touristy and, like so many others, prided itself on real Italian food with that great love and respect for ingredients. It ardently refused to modernise its menu and just did what it did well. It was also run by lovely people who always had time to talk without the hassle of tourists in a hurry.

A young waiter whom Jennifer didn't recognise, but quickly noticed was very good-looking, was getting that evening's tables ready outside on the street. Carlo had the stereotypical older Italian man's ample physique, not overly fat but having drunk plenty of good wine. This younger lad followed another stereotype – thin, well-muscled – and Jennifer couldn't help but enjoy looking at his bum as he bent over to clean the tables.

It was far too early for any customers to be there. The really touristy places had to keep serving all through the day and continuously into the evening. Tucked away like this, Carlo could afford to keep to the classic Italian eating hours of starting dinner late and going on into the evening. And, of course, serving good wine, Vin Santo and limoncello.

Halfway down the road Jennifer took a turn down an even quieter road. Dead reckoning told her it was going in roughly the right direction but for some reason she'd never been down it before. She normally liked to know exactly what was going on but for some reason, on that day, she felt like trying something new. Maybe it was a present to herself for being so well behaved at the fashion show, but she wanted to be a bit impulsive for once. She felt there might be something interesting down there that would be one of those serendipitous discoveries that happened in books.

Actually, most of the buildings seemed to be residential or businesses. One of the buildings had an understated sign saying 'Avvocato', lawyer, another said 'Contabile', accountant. Both were stylish-looking and looked appropriately expensive for a street this close to the city centre.

The street was quiet and there was no-one ahead of Jennifer so she could just enjoy the peacefully beautiful day and gently stroll her way in the general direction of home. She even started gently swinging her handbag, loosely held in her fingers.

Suddenly she felt a sharp tug at her hand. She instinctively tightened her grip on her handbag straps and looked towards the young man, who could have been called a boy, as he was grabbing at her bag. He wasn't looking back. He seemed intent on running past her and taking the bag. As she gripped harder and he ran on, her arm extended between them and he had to slow down. He looked back at her with cold determined eyes and used his free arm to push Jennifer's nearest shoulder hard away from him.

She lost her balance in her high heels and fell backwards towards the street surface. In the shock of trying to catch herself as she fell, she lost her grip on the bag. In the split second it took him to make her lose control he snatched the bag and ran right down the little street. By the time Jennifer landed on her backside he was already almost out of sight.

It was all over so fast and had happened without any warning; it was all Jennifer could do, sat unceremoniously in the middle of the now-deserted street, to work out what had just happened. Once she got her breath back she did a quick self-assessment and worked out that she wasn't actually hurt. One of her heels was broken and her bum felt a bit sore from the hard landing, but otherwise she was basically OK.

The bag was a bit irritating: the label and the cost didn't really worry her but she liked it and it suited her life. She had to think hard about how worried she should be about the contents. Luckily her mobile was in her dress pocket, a long-standing habit of hers; for some nagging reason she couldn't really find words for, she'd always felt the need to keep it separate from her other valuables. On reflection, she realised that the contents of the bag weren't too worrying either. She was always careful not to carry anything she didn't need. Important identifying documents were back at the apartment. No-one could get into the apartment without knowing the entry codes for the security system, and the twenty-four-hour security made her feel safe in case anyone tried to follow her.

There was a credit card and a bit of cash in her purse but even if they tried to use the card before she had a chance to cancel it, no-one could use the card without another code. In her head she could put the cash down to a lesson learned.

What really annoyed her was just how easily she had been defeated. The man had barely spent any time and he'd got exactly what he wanted. She had always refused to be considered weak but she'd been completely unable to stop him. She realised, as part of her self-assessment, that it was her pride that hurt more than anything else. She felt like she should have been stronger and, at that moment, as she got herself up, she vowed she would never be in that situation again. She would learn to fight back.

As she got up gingerly and moved to the edge of the road, she rang Mark to ask him to come with a non-broken pair of shoes. Despite all her assurances that she was basically OK, he went into panicked overdrive and sprinted as fast as he could with the first pair of shoes he could find.

No matter how much she tried to switch her brain off when she was on holiday, she couldn't help questioning the world that had just turned upside down on her. She started thinking about the thief. Why had he done it? In a sense she knew it didn't really matter. Whatever his reasons, it was theft. Jennifer refused to think of anything that could be considered an excuse, or to feel sorry for him, but she couldn't help thinking around the reason for it. Was it drugs? Was there some deep socio-economic reason behind his need? Was it desperation for food? Was it just good old-fashioned greed?

These were all good questions that people with degrees in relevant subjects needed to find answers to if anything was ever going to change. She felt like crying. She knew she couldn't change the reasons behind what had just happened and that frustrated her. Of course, deep down she knew her emotions were really about the bag snatch itself, her inability to stop it and the fact that she was sitting on her backside on a strange street. Fear was also creeping into her, which she really didn't like. Luckily for her sanity, Mark turned up and broke her thoughts.

"What the…?" Mark questioned as he came to a stop.

The panic had only grown in his head as he'd been sprinting faster and faster. When he saw her by the side of the road, all the images that had formed in his head of how she might look were thankfully disproved. She looked more annoyed than upset and there were no signs of the half-expected bruises and gushing blood.

"Let's talk when we get home," Jennifer replied as she changed her shoes and let Mark help her up.

Suddenly all her determination not to be seen as weak was overtaken by an overwhelming need for a cuddle. Once they got home, and without needing to be asked, Mark poured Jennifer the brandy she also badly needed.

Over dinner, Mark started the subject of what they ought to do about it but quickly realised two things: firstly, he realised that whilst he had been imagining all sorts of broken bones, his wife had been working the 'what nexts'; secondly, they both agreed that there was not much that could be done and the 'what nexts' were actually quite minimal.

Between that night and getting home to England she did work out something she could do, and sorted out some self-defence classes. Annoyingly, the first thing she was taught was that the safest thing to do if someone grabbed at your handbag was to let it go. She was hoping for some really kick-ass moves but she grudgingly had to admit that, at the end of the day, she was more important than the bag.

She did learn some defensive moves, mainly concentrating on getting out of a dangerous situation, and some of the more creative ways of hurting a, usually male, attacker if escaping wasn't an immediate option. She was a bit happier when she was taught how to use her knee to cause maximum pain to a man.

6

September

Sue and Jeff didn't get out cycling as often as they would have liked, but they got lucky with one very mild September weekend when they had very little else to do. They'd packed their bags and loaded the rack, then the bikes, on the back of the car on the Thursday evening and took it all to work the next day. That meant they could drive straight from work on the Friday afternoon. They found the drive out of the city annoyingly slow, even for a Friday, but did have to admit that their readiness to get away might relate to their desperate need to get away from the concrete jungle. Work hadn't been particularly bad that week compared to any other but they were all pretty depressing and even a short trip away was relished.

As soon as possible they were away from the city and having a lovely drive to the B&B in the middle of the beautiful and, crucially, hilly English countryside. Luckily the rest of the drive was uneventful and they got there in time for a pint or two in the village pub.

The village was a small classic British rural spot. It had a few more modern house at its edges and a centuries-old centre with the obligatory Norman church and small village green. With the bus stop, the respectfully tended stone war memorial, the little village shop and of course the pub, the picture-book likeness was complete. They'd even been able to keep an old-fashioned red cast-iron phone box by the green, but the keen-eyed could see that the modern version next to the bus stop was actually providing the service.

It was still just about nice enough to sit outside so, determined to stretch the summer out as long as possible, they both sat down at one of the picnic tables in the back garden. The garden was nicely kept, with the obligatory large grassy space for tables. The pub was a classically local limestone building that served really good local ale. Even though Sue normally stuck to wine, she was also quite capable of appreciating some of the local brew, especially when it was served by people who knew what they were doing.

Plenty of locals were enjoying the end of the week inside the pub, but the garden was largely empty apart from a group of twenty-year-olds, three boys and a girl, who were discussing the bike ride they were going on the next day as they drank their lemonades. Even though Sue and Jeff were there for the same reason, it was clear from the almost military-style planning the group seemed to be discussing that they were taking it a lot more seriously. No beers for the serious riders – that wasn't what they were there for. Sue and Jeff were there to enjoy the area and only put in what effort they were able to. The others were clearly there to cycle as hard and as far as they could.

The building's floodlighting meant they could stay there as it got dark. The treasured end of the summer was made even sweeter by appreciating the outside world. Someone obviously spent some time tending the garden's borders. Neither of them knew very much about gardening but they recognised a few classic herbaceous plants. The later-flowering ones still brought some lovely colour and smells to go with the good beer. They weren't going to drink too much before a cycling day but after another hard week the beer was hugely appreciated by both Jeff and Sue.

The B&B was a little twee for their personal taste – flowery bedsheets with a few more frilly trims on the bedclothes than they felt were needed; and the spare toilet roll, as far as they were concerned, did not need the crocheted lady's skirt to hide it. But it did its job. It gave them a pleasant place to stay ready for the real business of the weekend. Most importantly, it provided a very decent shower that they knew they would need after a hard day in the saddle.

The next morning they were at breakfast by seven so they could get some well-chosen calories into them and start out, by their definition, early. The local bacon and, sausages and the B&B's own eggs would have to wait for the next morning as they built up the carbs they needed. Happily, the bread was from the local bakery and the local jam made it all very lovely.

They had wondered if the group from the pub garden would be there but, on reflection, realised that they probably had a much earlier definition of early and had probably stayed in the much cheaper youth hostel near the edge of the village. They also imagined that they had had a far more practical breakfast that didn't warrant time spent enjoying it.

Sue and Jeff knew that they were very much part-time riders but they still knew they still had to do some stretching before they started. It may be that they were going to be a lot slower but they were still going up the same hills as the serious riders, and their muscles would still hurt if they got it wrong. Before they got properly started, they stopped at the village shop to get some food for lunch and some drinks to add to the water bottles they had already filled with tap water.

The village was in one of the many valley bottoms, with several miles of nearly flat road to cycle on before they started what they called 'proper ascents'. The road was quite quiet so they were able to start out side by side at a nice gentle pace, occasionally chatting as they went.

"Just breathe in that fresh air," Sue said through her smile after she took in a deep breath. There was very little wind so the late summer smells still came out of the village gardens. "I've no idea what those yellow flowers are but we should maybe get some for our garden."

"They've been tended, by the looks of it," Jeff replied. "One thing we rarely have time for, remember?"

"I know; I only said should, not could."

"By the way, I know we're supposed to be appreciating the countryside and all, but may I point out that your bum looks lovely in Lycra?"

"Pervert," Sue replied with a grin on her face that made it impossible to hide how much she enjoyed the flattery.

"I just figured that while I'm doing the red-blooded male thing, taking on nature, I'd do it properly and admire the woman I love."

"Really? If you were that red-blooded you'd be off with that group we saw last night, bombing around these hills, not pootling along with me."

"Yeah, also I wouldn't feel the need to do some more stretching so quickly after we started. Can we pull up at that lay-by ahead?"

Sue desperately tried to stop herself laughing too loudly; sometimes irony was so obvious it didn't need pointing out. Without another word they pulled into the lay-by and Jeff headed straight for a convenient lamp post. As soon as he stopped, Jeff laid his bike down and stretched his stiffening calf muscle.

"God, I feel like an amateur," he said as Sue joined him.

"Don't worry, love. Is this a private lamp post or can anyone join in?" she said as she stretched her own muscles.

They had been doing a few evening and lunchtime rides to build up to this weekend but they weren't sure it was enough. When they felt they'd done everything they could, they kissed and moved off.

They carried on for another half a mile and, just after the village petered out, spotted their turning to get into the proper countryside. The nice garden cultivation quickly disappeared and turned into a cross between agricultural cultivation and whatever nature decided to do. Firstly, it decided to stay fairly level and present a sweet little stream with an ancient-looking stone bridge to ride over. The pace was still slow enough for Sue to notice the ducks paddling on it. She made a mental note to herself that on another visit there would be duck-feeding opportunities. For the time being, however, nature was about to present them with something else to concentrate on.

The start of the climb was relatively benign, officially marked as 3.3%, or 1 in 30, as she preferred to think of it. She could cope with that.

Then nature decided to change tack. Benignness turned to malevolence as the slope along the road ahead began to rise to 1 in 5. Sue and Jeff took the next turning on the left, which took a gentler slope, winding more circuitously up the same hill. The 1 in 10 still felt hard work to them, and at that point the ride was starting to get more serious. The time for chat was on hold and they both needed to go at their own comfortable speed. Luckily for them, they actually matched speeds quite well. Sue's slim build meant her power-to-weight ratio wasn't far off Jeff's. He wasn't at all badly built but he was that bit stockier, and his leg muscles had more to pull up the hill. While she still could, Sue mentally noted the quality of his bum in Lycra.

They could cope with the steepness as long as they stayed in lower gears and weren't bothered about trying for any speed records. After a few more turns they eventually re-joined the steeper road, and for the last little bit the slope became 1 in not very many at all. It was hard work, but the struggling would have been bearable if it hadn't been for the group from the pub the night before overtaking them, with annoying ease, at the steepest part.

When they got to the top of that first hill they both stopped and stood astride their bikes for a very welcome chance to catch their breath, drink some water and admire the view. Given the infrequency with which they did this, the first swig was essential, the second badly needed and the third barely noticeable. The trip down the other side of that first hill was much gentler but still enjoyable. They both enjoyed cutting through the still air without having to do the work – gravity did it for them. The gentleness of the slopes and the curves on that road meant they weren't at all nervous about freewheeling down.

After another couple of hills, again taking the slightly gentler routes on the way up and freewheeling on the way down, they stopped for a badly needed lunch break at the top of a particularly high hill. Being the consummate gadget lover, Jeff checked his speedometer, which kept track of average and maximum speeds. He was happy to note that, at best, he had managed 32 miles per hour, which must have been down the 1 in 6 slope descending their second hill.

Once they'd sat astride their bikes for a few minutes, recovering the ability to talk, they both got off, laid the bikes on the ground by the side of the road and sat down. Jeff started to get their lunch out of his small saddle bag. It was just big enough to hold one half-litre bottle of water, their food and a spare inner tyre with the tools needed in case of a puncture.

"We do this for fun, right?" Sue questioned when she was finally able to breathe.

"Look at the view. We wouldn't get this view without the ride."

"They invented cars and motorbikes and things so people could get to the view without the stress."

"Yeah, but listen to the quietness. We wouldn't get that if there were cars around."

"I know. I'll feel a lot happier about the view once I've eaten something. Pass me one of those bananas, please."

"With you on that." And with gratitude they tucked into the conveniently self-packaged source of nutrition they so badly needed.

Once they had quickly and silently finished the fruit, they went on to the only slightly melted chocolate bars.

"I bet that group doesn't have melted chocolate," Jeff said with a resigned sigh.

"They probably stocked up on mint cake, or something else with carefully calculated non-melty calories. You're right, though. The view is lovely."

They both fell silent again and took some time to enjoy the sun on their faces and, indeed, the view. They both took long deep breaths and enjoyed the freshness and clearness of the air.

"Why don't we do this more often?" Jeff asked.

"Can I refer the honourable gentleman to the earlier feeling in his legs as he got to the top of the hill?"

"I know, but my question still stands. There is so much else to do that isn't to do with Cuthbert's. Why don't we do more of it?"

"Oi! We had a moratorium on talking about work, remember? Don't spoil all this."

"I know. I'm sorry. My brain is zizzing all around and inevitably ended up comparing this to that place."

"Ssshhh!" Sue commanded, and leant over to kiss him. They both smiled and spent some more time relaxing.

"Thanks a bunch," Sue declared after a few minutes. "Now I'm thinking of the best way of killing the ice queen."

"A little excessive, don't you think? How on earth do you get from this loveliness to premeditated murder? Or don't I want to know?"

"It has something to do with breathing in the lovely air, using breaths which are nice and deep and even, then

I jumped to thinking about snow, which got me to the ice queen. My brain's a worrying place sometimes."

"Isn't the snow supposed to be crisp and deep and even?"

"Close enough. Anyway, she gets her shirts ironed and starched so well they look crisp."

"Nice. Anyway, what's with the murder thing?" he asked, looking around to make sure the hills really were as empty as they thought. "I know we don't like them but I can see our lives suffering if either of us gets done for killing the woman."

"Don't worry, it's only a thought. I'm sure I read something once that said it's physiologically healthy to think about killing your boss. I mean, I'd obviously never do it, but it must be good to vent your angst against someone who causes so much hassle."

The whole tone of the conversation changed as they laughed at that remark. All of a sudden the day wasn't spoilt by Jeff's earlier comment, and they spent some time enjoying the loveliness whilst trying to think of the most ridiculous way to kill Francesca. To ensure equality in the workplace, they included ways of killing TF Junior as well.

"They both drink that hideously strong poncy coffee; you know, the stuff you could stand a spoon up in, if it didn't dissolve the spoon," Sue started.

"Yeah, so?" Jeff responded.

"So, I bet it would hide the flavour of a poison perfectly."

"He's too precious about his supply. We would never get near enough to it to lace it properly."

Sue paused and did some more view appreciating. After a few minutes she voiced a thought. "How about coating his mug in something? As long as it didn't look obvious he would just add the coffee to it."

"Wouldn't work. He even locks up his poncy cups in his office cupboard. Either he regards the common area too common for his precious crockery or he doesn't trust us."

"She's the same, come to think of it. Are they worried about breakages or poisoning?"

"Who'd think such a thing? Shocking!" They both laughed and continued resting, breathing the air and occasionally plotting.

When they felt ready they started off on the next leg of their ride, still with silly smiles on their faces, which only lasted to the next steep, by their definition, ascent. As far as they were concerned, another of the positive effects of the strenuous ascent to the top was the fun of another descent. Their smiles changed slightly, from silly to joyous, as they freewheeled through the refreshing air to the bottom.

The grins lasted even longer as the route they'd chosen took them along a stunning valley bottom, past another duck-filled stream. They reached another pretty little village and stopped outside the local café for some much appreciated lunch. They refilled their water bottles and set off again.

They stopped a few more times, to rest and drink some more. They were starting to really feel their tiredness, so conversation barely happened. They went up and down the slightly more gentle routes of a few more hills and ended the day with a final descent almost straight into the village they were staying in. Jeff was pleased to note that the tally on his gizmo showed they had done 38.9 miles, and he'd maxed out at 37 miles per hour, which he proudly announced to Sue, and anyone else nearby, as they parked their bikes up at the B&B. As predicted, the shower they almost fell into as soon as they got back to their room was hugely appreciated, and then they went for a badly needed dinner in the village pub.

As soon as they got to the pub they realised that what they really needed, or at least wanted, badly, was a pint each. Almost before they'd given their food order, the pints were drunk, feeling like they didn't even touch the sides as they went. Jeff's mixed grill and Sue's burger with chips may not have been of the greatest sophistication but their need for a substantial meal each was so great that it was irrelevant. They switched to lemonade and picked a table to wait for their food.

After they finished their meals at the hard-chaired pub tables, they took their second pints to the comfy chairs in the corner of the room. As it happened, it was quieter there, which suited them fine.

They sat supping their pints for a few minutes. It quickly became obvious to Sue, as soon as their need for calories had been satisfied, that there was something else on Jeff's mind. She reached across and gently squeezed his hand.

"I just can't stop asking myself the same question," Jeff quietly said as he responded by putting his other hand over both and squeezing back. "What are we doing still working there?"

"We've been over this so many times," Sue answered, not sounding at all judgemental or bored with the old conversation one or other of them had started at various times over the previous few years. Periodically, they almost seemed to take it in turns to doubt whether they were making the right decisions. This time it was Sue's turn to look at the practical side of things. "It's a very good question, and I guess it's always worth making sure nothing has changed – but you know the reasons. And they are still as strong as ever."

"I'm not sure they are, or at least not all of them."

Sue took another sip of her beer and looked quizzically at Jeff.

He tried to answer her unspoken invitation to elaborate. "What's really stopping us from taking all the stuff we've got – you know, the skills and... well, stuff – and doing something else with it? Surely we've got enough to be useful by now?"

"Personally I think there is more 'stuff', as you call it, to get. Just think of the arsehole management skills we're learning, and the lessons on 'how not to do it'. That's got to be saleable, don't you think? "And how about the people we do care about? Yeah, OK, Cuthbert's long since stopped being the place we used to love working at but, with a few notable exceptions, as per the plans we made today, we love the people."

"It has to end one day. The TFs are driving the firm into the ground."

"And we can help try to stop the suffering as much as possible."

"Haven't we done enough? We're never going to get the thanks we deserve."

"We don't stick around for gratitude. Or at least I didn't think we did."

Jeff suddenly looked like a told-off schoolboy. "I'm sorry. I know that sounded really spoilt-brattish. It's just that sometimes I feel like I've given the place more of me than is healthy. I feel like there's a whole world out there to enjoy and I'm stuck propping up something that is going to die one day anyway."

"I know it's hard sometimes; dear God, do I know. My life would definitely be happier without the ice queen in it. But somehow I just don't feel ready to stop yet. Maybe it's some weird kind of institutionalisation... or bizarre Stockholm syndrome thing. NO!" She stopped herself suddenly, slapping her spare hand down onto her chair arm in mock anger. "That would mean I had some kind of emotional attachment to her. Yeuch!" She shuddered slightly and drank some more beer.

"If that's true it must be time to get out." Jeff smiled, glad to have his sour mood broken by Sue's comedy-style reaction.

After some more beer Sue carried on with the lighter tone she was glad to have regained. "They're a nightmare to work for, yes. The company's being destroyed, yes. Some of the best people have already left, totally know that. But really, I think there are some good sides to the life we have. At the end of the day I think there is more of that 'stuff' you mentioned earlier we can get out of them. Don't you think?"

"I see what you're saying, and I know how important it is to keep an eye on the bad guys. But will you agree to at least keeping an eye on our own well-being?"

"Agreed," Sue said, raising her glass to the deal.

They clinked beer glasses, finished their beers and then went back to the B&B for some very rapidly achieved sleep.

The Sunday morning breakfast was much enjoyed before heading back to normal life. They both agreed that the big questions could wait for a while; but, if they were both being honest, there were nagging doubts in the backs of their minds.

7

"Hello?" Sue answered her mobile phone with that quizzical tone people use when they either don't recognise the number or they see that it is a call from an unexpected number. She must have given this number to the caller but she could not remember when.

"*Guten morgen.* Is it possible to speak to you in the moment?" the Germanic voice asked in not-quite-perfect English.

"Actually, this will have to be quick as I'm just going into a meeting. What could possibly be this important?" Sue answered, turning her head away from anyone who might overhear.

She was sitting at her desk but the office door was open and Francesca would frown at this private call. Actually, everyone else was far too busy to notice what Sue was doing so she was able to have the conversation in complete privacy. No-one even noticed as she hurriedly left the building while texting Jeff to ring her urgently.

Jeff was able to leave his office without fuss, knowing TF Junior was off on some jolly that day. It was a shock when he nearly bumped into Junior by the main office door.

What?! Jeff thought to himself as he quickly twisted to avoid their shoulders colliding. *I thought you were in Spain!* The sudden shock in the middle of an unexpectedly needed action threw him off-balance for a moment. *Calm down. You've got stuff to do.*

"Sorry. Family emergency. Got to go. I've already checked the finance report's gone off."

Actually, Junior didn't even seem to hear him, or even pay any attention to him at all, so Jeff was able to get out of the building practically unnoticed.

Two hours later, Sue and Jeff were hurriedly walking into their respective toilets at their regular airport, still wearing the work suits they had been in all day. Sue walked into one of the few free cubicles with her overnight bag, past the oblivious stressed travellers who were frantically sorting themselves out before joining the long check-in queues.

As soon as the door was locked she checked that the floor wasn't too dirty before putting her overnight bag next to the toilet. She took off the cream-coloured lightweight coat she was wearing. It had felt a bit chilly outside but she hadn't wanted to be weighed down by a bulky winter coat, so she'd put up with it while she had to. She hung it on the hook on the back of the door, followed by the blue lightweight cardigan she'd grabbed from home when she'd picked up the bag.

She took a baby wipe out of the packet she always kept in the bag and wiped the top of the seat lid. It may not have been that dirty but her skirt was clean on that morning and she wanted to make sure it stayed that way. She then dried it off with a tissue she also kept handy. Maybe there was more fastidiousness in her than she cared to admit, or maybe she had spent enough time in public toilets to be cautious.

She sat down, took off her court shoes and unbuttoned her blouse. She stood back up to hang her blouse over her cardigan. She unbuttoned and unzipped her skirt and, holding the waistband so it didn't drop to the floor, stepped out of it. She then folded it neatly and put it on top of the seat. Trying desperately to move fast but not put her thumb through her flesh-coloured tights, she then removed them. They joined the pile as neatly as is ever possible to fold tights. Then her Marks & Spencer matching underwear was placed on the pile. She was left standing completely naked surrounded by the panicky sounds going on outside of her cubicle.

Partly out of the need for efficiency and largely because she was feeling cold, she then took her other pile of clothes out of her overnight bag. She started by putting on her matching silk bra, camisole and briefs, then her silk Armani blouse and complimentary wide-leg trousers, finishing with socks and high-heeled ankle boots. After putting her other clothes in the overnight bag she sat back down and took out her matching handbag. She released her ponytail and brushed her neatly bobbed, shoulder-length hair, then put on her simple but expensive headband and eye and lip make-up. Her simple half-carat diamond stud earrings finished the look.

She took her coat off the hook and turned it inside out. She then put on her dark blue coat, making sure the collar was turned to show the cream detailing. When she was satisfied, Jennifer walked calmly past those other frantic travellers and out of the toilet towards her husband Mark, who had changed into his slim-fit Armani jeans and open-collared striped shirt. As she walked, her mobile rang again and the first Mark heard was:

"Look, I'm really sorry, Francesca. My mum's been taken into hospital and I've had to go at short notice. All the monthly reports are done and in your inbox, and the team is perfectly able to cope without me. I'll be back as soon as possible, probably no more than a few days. I have to go, they're ready with her medication," Sue said as she hung up.

"That is so much easier when I can't see her stroppy face," Jennifer said as they walked past those frantic-looking check-in queues and walked straight up to the first-class desk.

Three hours later Jennifer and Mark Page walked into their bank and handed Herr Gyger the paperwork he needed. The bank's information storage had been updated and, with profuse apologies, the bank manager explained that they were not able to find the records of the Pages' proof of original financial source.

"We expect better service from a bank with your reputation," Mark said. "We had to deal with this ourselves. Dropping our commitments to get here at short notice is not a trivial exercise, especially as you saw the will and the trust agreement when we opened the account. What on earth has gone wrong?"

"I am so sorry," Herr Gyger said with an apologetic half bow. "Our internal IT system has just been replaced with some new, supposedly more efficient, database manager, and the record of having seen the documentation has been lost for your account. Everything has become... what's the English phrase?... 'twisty'."

"What?!" Mark snapped, suddenly changing from businesslike listening mode to hard cold stare. Jennifer knew him well enough to know that for some reason his raised shoulders showed an even more increased stress level.

"I'm sorry," continued Herr Gyger, "I think I meant 'twisted'."

Mark seemed to smile to himself and continued listening.

"But why us and why such urgency?" Jennifer demanded to know.

"Your first question I am afraid I cannot answer; as for the second question, we are regularly audited and have to prove we are satisfied with our knowledge of the legality of the money. Also, the latest investments you requested require similar information and there was a deadline on the most attractive terms. The bank will of course compensate you for the inconvenience caused."

"The money isn't the problem," Mark responded sharply, "it's simply the timing which has caused problems. Luckily our usual hotel is able to accommodate us tonight, and if we are finished we would like to go."

"Please would you sign to say that you have shown us the true documents? Then all is complete."

They only stayed one night, worried that it would look odd if they suddenly cancelled the Saturday night dinner they had planned with Rob. That evening Jennifer and Mark sat in near silence, eating dinner in the usual hotel dining room, only asking for the condiments to be passed when they needed them. They weren't at all annoyed with each other but they both knew that sudden, unexpected events, like the bank needing documents out of the blue, had a tendency to make them pause and question what they were doing.

PART II

WHY and ELSE-WHY?

Six and a half years earlier

8

April

Everything seemed as it should be. Sue and Jeff had been married for a year and been living together for two years in a rented two-bedroom flat, in a square red-brick block, with five other couples in identical flats. Everyone rented so there hadn't been much personalisation of the drab, neutral décor, apart from a few posters, put up carefully so they wouldn't lose their deposit. They were all young professionals who got on OK when they said hello in the shared corridors. They were all near the beginning of their careers in a sizeable city and were there temporarily, either because they suited small-scale single living or because they just couldn't afford to move onto the housing chain yet.

They were both moving up in their own section of Cuthbert's structure, both very good at their jobs. They showed a really good balance between having potential to go into management and knowing what was going on where the real work was done.

Sue and Jeff had had several conversations questioning whether two secular people, who never had a strong wish to have children, really needed to be married, but they had decided they wanted to. They both wanted – in fact, they both felt they needed – some formal commitment in their lives, partly to make up for what had been difficult earlier times. Actually, it turned out that both the marriage and a habit they'd quickly developed of thoroughly discussing things came in very useful.

One fairly ordinary Friday evening Sue was sitting in the living room with a glass of nice but cheap red wine and one of her favourite films, making comfortable use of the fact that Jeff was out. He was with his colleagues, saying goodbye to one of the longest-serving employees of Cuthbert's IT department.

Terry was one of those people who had been around for so long that he knew the company and the IT systems it used from the bottom up. He'd refused point blank to try for any promotions to management roles and consequently wasn't very high up in the company structure. He was far more interested in actually doing the job than talking about it. In fact, he'd had a hand in building most of the IT and had one of those brains that the more sensible remaining staff wanted to download before he left.

The problem from Terry's point of view was that not everyone was that sensible, and he knew the management wanted to change things in ways that wouldn't work, and he'd had enough. He was getting on and decided that life was too short to spend the rest of it having pointless arguments with, as he saw it, suits full of nothing.

There had been the usual formal parting at work, with everyone from his department, and quite a few others, gathered to hear their manager reciting polite compliments about Terry and giving him the obligatory leaving presents.

Of course, the management had been useless at knowing what to get Terry; they didn't really know him. It was the more junior members of staff who knew exactly which single malt whisky was his favourite.

The evening started in a nice Italian restaurant that Terry had suggested, and then a few of the group, the ones with young children, said their goodbyes. The rest moved to a nice local real ale pub, the sort of place where there was no music and you could sit down and have a conversation. This was clearly not what the younger team members wanted. They were far more interested in cheaper beer and plenty of up-to-date music, so as soon as they politely could they said their goodbyes and headed for the trendier parts of the city. This just left Jeff and Terry enjoying the obviously dying art of conversation.

They started off talking about the relative merits of rugby union and rugby league. Terry was a proud Yorkshireman and in his youth had been an enthusiastic rugby league player. His short, athletic build made him a perfect, or at least quite good, scrum half. Once he got the ball, he had the speed and agility to run into the gaps his bigger teammates had made and move the ball forward. His analytical mind, judging what was needed to make the game go well, later came in useful in the IT world. He had never been a great player but he was good enough for a local amateur team and carried on playing into his early thirties.

Unlike some of his teammates he'd never been a volume drinker – his father had taught him about quality over quantity – so keeping relatively slim was never a problem. As he got older his body never really deteriorated, even in later years, so he still had that build. Obviously he had very strong opinions on which rugby code was better. Jeff, who didn't actually care, enjoyed playing devil's advocate, and the conversation got quite heated, in a very friendly and slightly alcohol-fuelled way.

Despite their best efforts they inevitably found themselves talking about work and all the management-induced stress.

"They are going to find themselves in deep trouble if they don't start recognising and listening to the knowledge and talent they have on their doorstep," Terry said with a very matter-of-fact resignation. He was never one of those moany 'the world's about to end' types but he wasn't afraid to say what he saw. He also wasn't a hypocrite and had said as much to his management, which had led to many arguments.

"I know we said it formally before but it's absolutely true that they never should have let you go," Jeff replied.

"They would have had to tie me to the chair. You know, I just couldn't be doing with all the arguments. They have a perfectly good working system and as long as they insist on crowbarring in their precious new pile of shiny, useless rubbish, my prediction is that life is going to get a lot harder than it has to be."

By this point the several glasses of wine over dinner and several pints of delicious real ale were starting to make Terry feel a lot more relaxed about venting his views, and the fact that he was leaving meant he was even more verbal than normal. The rugby conversation had also loosened up his arguing juices.

"My advice to you is to do two things: brush up your CV and start running before it all goes hideously wrong."

"It won't be that bad, surely."

"I've seen it before. The shiny new system won't work. It won't interface properly with what we've built. And guess who'll be blamed. I'll give you a clue: their name won't end with Teatherstone-Fox."

"But how will that look to a new prospective employer – I left just before it all went wrong?"

That made Terry smile a bit as he punctuated the conversation with another sip of beer.

"OK, if you won't do the least stupid thing, you'll have to get yourself well bedded in, you mark my words, young grasshopper," Terry predicted in equally mock Eastern wisdom, stroking an imaginary long goatee beard. Jeff was a little too young to get the 1970s' kung fu reference but Terry had called him that so often it had become a running joke.

Jeff laughed and grabbed the two empty pint glasses as he stood up. "I take it the old wise one would like another?"

"Less of the old. Sixty is the new fifty, remember? Same again, please. I've got a taste for that one."

When Jeff got back he had clearly been thinking further on the subject.

"How d'you mean, bedded in?"

"My advice is that you should get to know the software so well that when the interface points fail to work, because they've insisted on using the proverbial sledgehammer to crack the proverbial nut, you'll know how to patch the wounds. You'll need to find every nook and cranny to even find the wounds. When it all goes wrong you could make yourself invaluable by finding the solution somewhere in the code."

"I helped build the new system, remember; I already know it inside out!" Jeff was mildly miffed at the suggestion that he didn't know the system he had designed.

"I'm not suggesting you don't know your stuff. Don't forget that before you got involved we built a preliminary version to try out various techniques. Some of them worked so well that we kept the links to them and never wrote replacements. They're not that obvious but if you do a bit of digging you'll find them. They also do a shoddy job of connecting to TF Junior's new and sexy system, especially those precious, proprietary bits that only the honoured few are supposed to touch."

"I thought I knew everything there was to know about it."

"Don't beat yourself up. In my experience all major IT systems have some code that most people never look at. Most of the time they run smoothly but if you're not careful they can cause unpredicted problems, especially when you link them to new, hideously messy stuff."

"So, what you're saying is either I cut and run, or I spend my career groping around shoddy code to find places to put sticking plasters."

"It might not be as bad as you think. It's amazing what little gems you might find buried somewhere in the code, especially when you follow the money."

He paused for a moment while he took another very much appreciated sip of beer. "Could get tricky, I suppose, if they go for the dreaded 'O' word."

"Now what are you on about?" Jeff asked, looking very confused. The IT world was full of abbreviations and jargon but that was a new one on him.

"Outsourcing, don't you remember? Despite their promises to stay faithful to Cuthbert's ethos, outsourcing is the new buzz word. My prediction, for what it's worth, is that they'll get rid of all the people who know the company and the systems inside out and replace them with external types who don't. They're often the first people to go. But then," another bit of beer seemed to help his thoughts, "maybe they have reason to hang on to IT. I don't know." His brain clearly wandered off somewhere Jeff knew nothing about.

"Maybe. If you've managed to get that cynical, you've definitely spent too much of your life worrying about work."

"You're not wrong. It's definitely time for a change."

"What are you going to do instead?" Jeff wondered what life was like when work didn't dominate everything.

"Travel. There's a whole world out there, and the nice thing about not having had a life for so long is that I've managed to save up a nice travel pot."

The conversation drifted off into plans that Terry had made to visit places he'd always wanted to see and Jeff could only dream about. Eventually the pub's bell announced that it was time to head off and, after a very firm goodbye handshake, both wishing the other all the best, they headed for their separate buses.

*

"How was your evening?" Sue asked when Jeff eventually got home and kissed the top of her head.

"Interesting. We are definitely going to miss Terry far more than management realises," Jeff announced with that slight lilt that Sue knew meant he certainly wasn't hammered but was definitely on the merry side.

"I don't know about you but my day is definitely over," he added as he headed for the bedroom.

Sue had only just finished her third glass of wine and another much-loved film so she followed Jeff towards bed and was happy to find that, despite the ale, the day wasn't quite over.

Jeff was surprised to wake up what felt like the next morning; at least, 9am on a Saturday seemed quite early to someone with no kids who'd been out drinking late the night before. What surprised him more was the fact that he actually felt far more awake than he deserved to. Sue was still asleep so he quietly got out of bed, grabbed his clothes and got dressed in the bathroom.

While he was making himself an instant coffee, Jeff thought back to the previous night's conversation. He realised that he was more bothered than he'd thought about part of it. He couldn't help the nagging feeling in the back of his mind that he'd been accused of not completely knowing a system he was quite proud of.

As he started drinking the coffee at their little kitchen table he realised that that wasn't really what was bothering him. He'd always had a lot of time for Terry and it didn't take long to remember that the feeling was mutual. It just irritated him that there was something in what Terry said that seemed to suggest that things went on 'somewhere in the code', as Terry had described it, that he didn't know about.

He took his coffee into the spare room that they'd set up as a home office and logged onto his work computer. The new bosses pretty much expected the IT staff to be willing to work seven days a week, so the remote access network was already set up and Jeff could easily get to all of the systems.

As he looked through the routines that had been written in-house, everything looked to be as it should, which was a relief given that he'd designed a lot of it and had been a part of the code-writing team. The main parts were all about the website, where people could choose their shopping, and that was as expected; the warehousing, likewise; compiling the shopping lists, again fine; taking the payments, crucial, and again as expected. In fact, most of the payment processes were sorted by the bank so they shouldn't have held any surprises.

Data was saying the expected things, like how long food products like pasta could be stored for, which linked to the warehousing database telling the central depot that the local shop was running low on pasta, and so on. Everything seemed to make sense.

Then Jeff remembered another curious remark Terry had made.

"Follow the money."

"Follow what money?" Sue asked from the spare room door, making Jeff nearly jump out of his skin.

She'd got out of bed, been to the loo and even got herself a cup of coffee without him noticing. Which was surprising considering the paper-thin internal walls in the flat.

"Did I say that out loud?" Jeff asked once he had calmed down.

"Yes, dear. Surely you can't be working this early on a Saturday morning?"

"Not really. It's just something odd Terry said last night that made me think."

"Well, I'll leave you to it. I've got some calls to make," she said as she wandered off to the living room.

Jeff smiled at his wife's understanding and looked back at the computer screen. He started wondering about the money and why that should be any different to any other bit of data. The value of the pasta was just another piece of information that got added to the shopping list, and the bank got told the total amount to take out of the shopper's account. A dig around the code, including a few old routines, proved that.

In fact, the supermarket didn't really see most of the money. The banks took care of that end of things. Then he remembered the direct debits. As well as the ethically sourced groceries, Cuthbert's also sold equally ethical financial products, loans and insurance products of various kinds. The whole thing could be set up online, including regular direct debits for the premiums. Generally the customers then forgot about it unless something went wrong, when they would phone Sue's service centre to make a complaint. As expected, they had always prided themselves on great service.

Jeff started carefully looking through the programs related to the financial stuff. This was where TF Junior had brought in the unpopular software packages that didn't really do the job very well. They just about worked but kept going wrong, and only TF Junior, who had heavily protected access to the code, seemed to be able to fix it. The private company that provided the software kept a strong clause in the contract that meant that only certain named people, such as TF Junior, were legally allowed to touch it.

Terry's name had also been on that list, and as soon as he let it be known he was leaving he got Jeff on it as well as he was clearly the most suitable to take over his work. Jeff had had a cursory look over it when it became part of his remit. It did a very specific job that never needed to be touched again, so he had pretty much ignored it since then. When he started looking back over it on that Saturday morning, all seemed to make sense. All of the relevant banks electronically talked to each other, exchanged the relevant details and transferred the right amounts of money to Cuthbert's' bank account. Cuthbert's kept their cut, transferred it to a dedicated account, and the rest got paid to the insurance provider.

Using his favourite metaphor, one he frequently used when describing the system to non-IT-minded people, the pasta was bought, cooked and mixed with the appropriate sauce. All seemed as it should be. That was the problem. The more he looked, the more frustrated he got trying to find this seemingly mythical thing that was supposed to be 'somewhere in the code'. He remembered Terry's other phrase and it didn't seem to help at all.

"What do you mean 'somewhere in the code', you git? Why couldn't you say something useful like where?!" Somehow, deep in his mind, his yelling at the computer screen gave him some kind of psychic channel directly to Terry.

"Who are you talking to?" Sue asked from the door, an expression somewhere between amused and bemused on her face. "Do you want some lunch?"

"Will you please stop doing that to me?" Jeff responded once he had finished jumping out of his skin again. His bum and his bladder then realised that he had been sitting still for several hours, and he decided he needed a break.

Not much was said while Sue got a pizza out of the freezer and put it in the oven.

"You're not much of a conversationalist today," Sue announced while they munched through their lunch.

"I'm sorry, love," Jeff replied, looking up from the bit of the floor he'd been staring at intently. "Terry said something odd last night that got me thinking. I just need some time staring at software to try to understand it. I'm not much of a husband today but, trust me, I'll be less of one if I don't work out what's going on."

"Don't worry. I'll just go out to the shops and spend some of the money we don't have."

Jeff smiled, knowing that Sue was the more sensible one. He got up, kissed his wife on the top of her head, grabbed the rest of his pizza and went back to the computer.

Taking another bite of the rapidly cooling pizza, Jeff carried on going through the external bit of the software. He realised that he'd been guilty of making assumptions about how it should work, so he started at the beginning and pedantically worked his way through it. This took some serious concentration. It all seemed to make sense until suddenly he spotted one tiny line of code that had no place there.

At the beginning of this particular routine, Cuthbert's share of the direct debit insurance takings, the correct share, came in. As with all good code it was given a sensible name which made it obvious what it was. At the end, the same amount of money went out, to Cuthbert's bank account. Somewhere, buried in all that code, the money changed name.

What started out as something called ins_dd_mTot_ ptProf, the finance department's term for the total monthly pre-tax profit Cuthbert's received from the insurance direct debits, became ins_dd_rnTot_ptProf. It took Jeff a few moments of staring to work out what didn't quite look right. Anyone being anything less than thoroughly pedantic would have missed it. Anyone not understanding what was going on might have thought it was a typo. Jeff had never really paid attention to how much the combination of 'r' and 'n' right next to each other looked like an 'm'.

"That explains his stupid font thing!" Jeff said out loud.

Normally, programmers wouldn't have a problem with this. They should use a font that made things clear. But TF Junior, for a reason only he understood, insisted that the new shiny software was presented in a font that helped disguise the difference. Things that previously seemed trivial, or at least only a little annoying, started to fit together in Jeff's mind.

'mTot' was the monthly total. Twelve of them would add up to yTot, the yearly total. He had no idea what 'r' followed by 'n' followed by 'Tot' was. A few seconds later, when he did get it, it became blatantly obvious what it meant. The name change meant that there were two variables, both of which said they held the takings at the same time. Further down the same routine, the original variable, 'mTot', was sent to the routine that managed the transfer to Cuthbert's bank. Jeff followed the link and, somewhere further down that same routine, again buried, that amount was set as zero. Straight away Jeff realised this meant that the original name no longer had any money associated with it. It was all associated with the new name. The pasta sauce had changed from being a lovely rich tomato, garlic and herb ragu to nothing more than fresh air.

Near the end, the 'money', with its proper name, got sent to a different part of the system, which talked to their bank. Between the name change and the proper transfer, again buried amongst expected software, the money with the new name, the 'rnTot', was sent to a completely different part of the system that, Jeff confirmed after some more searching, sent it to some other company that Jeff had never heard of. That metaphorical ragu pasta sauce defied gravity, and halfway between the pot and the bowl got diverted to a different bowl of pasta on a different table, in a different dining room!

It was simply brilliant. Actually, Jeff realised, it was brilliantly simple. Some more digging proved that, due to the way the change was done, Cuthbert's bank thought that the amount of money it received was correct, even though it was actually being diverted. The same thing was done to the direct debit repayments from the loan business.

Something still didn't feel right but Jeff couldn't quite put his finger on it. The product provider got all the money it was expecting. The customers got the product they expected. It was only Cuthbert's that was missing out.

The original question had been answered. Jeff now knew what was going on, and some of the how, but he was convinced there were other questions that needed answering.

He was convinced they were important questions. He just had absolutely no idea what they were. While he pondered what he was not getting, he reached for his very cold slice of pizza.

9

A week later

The following weekend was Sue's turn to meet up with an ex-colleague. Gina had left Cuthbert's about six months earlier, having been the service centre manager for years, and moved to a new management job in London. Gina and Sue had kept in touch, so when Sue had to go to a meeting in the Teatherstone-Fox headquarters in London she took the chance to see Gina, and also have a cheap place to stay overnight.

When Gina left, Sue was promoted from assistant manager to branch manager. Of course, the TF Group didn't want what had become provincial staff to have senior management titles because that might encourage them to forget who was really in charge now. Not that the amount of work decreased. In fact, especially with the extra meetings, it went up.

The afternoon's meeting had been just as useless as Sue had expected. In the time since TF Senior had taken control of the company, she had come to know that meetings with his type were very one-way, with lots of pretending to listen, saying 'the right things' and completely false pleasantries.

Jeff had already had his version, but this time she had to go through the pretence.

The meeting took place in one of the swish-looking corporate boardrooms in the main Teatherstone-Fox headquarters. In the old Cuthbert's meeting rooms there had been an informal collection of tables that used to be arranged whichever way worked best, with comfortable but practical chairs. The Teatherstone-Fox room more resembled every stereotype of the harsh corporate boardroom. There was a single, large, expensive glass and metal framed board table, with a deliberately designed 'head' where the indisputable bosses held court. The difference between the old local meeting room and this one was made even more obvious by the cushioned, back-supporting business chairs for the bosses and the hard and stylish, but seriously uncomfortable, chairs for everyone else. Instead of the charming historical photos of old Cuthbert's shops through the ages, there were abstract paintings of coloured lines that were somehow both harsh and bland 'contemporary corporate art'.

The head of the austere board table was of course occupied by John Teatherstone-Fox, taking up the main centre spot, his son Nicholas sat to his left, and they were flanked by two accountants who never got introduced. At this meeting they were also joined by a very stylishly dressed thirty-something woman who, again, did not get introduced.

The meeting was supposed to be about 'brainstorming ideas for maximising the potential of the business', but in actual fact John TF, and only he, rambled on to all of the branch managers, with the notable exception of the IT department, about how all their opinions were valued and they were keeping a completely open mind. There was stuff about auditing to 'determine the measurables within the company'. Something about continuing the optimisation-oriented restructuring. There was other stuff too but people switched off after the first half hour. It was only for the last ten minutes of the meeting that they opened the floor to 'suggestions'.

"Your opinions are important to us," TF said with a tone that tried to sound sincere but that everyone had learned meant nothing, "so please don't be afraid to sock it to us," he finished, with a completely failed attempt at lightening the mood.

Not for the first, or last, time, Sue wondered if the stereotypical 'how to sound like a good manager while actually not caring at all' act was deliberate. Maybe he actually thought he was funny. Maybe he actually thought that was how people in their business spoke. Maybe there was a part of the business world that did actually talk like that and she just hadn't experienced it. Whatever the reason, she did know enough to know that saying anything would be pretty pointless. Her conversations with Jeff, and others, had taught her that the Teatherstone-Fox Group was clearly going to make its mark irrespective of trivial staff members' opinions. She also knew they would regard her as being relatively new to her 'management' post, so she wouldn't have had the confidence to say anything anyway.

Nobody else said much, except Greg, the branch manager of the distribution department, who was well known throughout the company as being a straight talker, and he asked the question everyone else was afraid to mention.

"Look, for all your fine words, there is real worry on the ground about whether your definition of 'maximising potential' is going to include outsourcing our jobs."

Greg had always been very honest; he was getting on in years and as he got closer to retirement he got even less afraid to say what he believed had to be said.

"When we merged with Cuthbert's," John TF replied, with a word everyone knew was a thinly veiled euphemism for 'took over', "we made a promise that we would do everything within our power to keep jobs local wherever possible. We will stand by that promise, especially while the work you do continues to be of the high quality we know you are capable of. Now, I think we have kept you long enough for a Friday afternoon, so thank you for your valuable input, which we will take on board."

With that, John TF and the rest of the headquarters staff got up and speedily left the room, ending the meeting in no uncertain terms. There was little doubt that they had planned the meeting for a Friday afternoon so they could easily do just that.

*

"How was the meeting?" Gina asked as she handed Sue the large glass of red wine that was sitting ready at the West End pub bar.

"They said all the right words," Sue answered, looking cynical and a bit tired. "The question is, does anyone believe them? Anyway, happy birthday." They clinked glasses and both took well-needed mouthfuls.

"Thank you. I know I started it but let's have a ban on talking about those lying bastards for the rest of my birthday."

"Deal," Sue agreed, raising her glass for another toast. "How's the new job going?"

"Great. It turns out that managing a team of public-facing staff in the telecoms sector has a lot in common with the old job. Once I climbed that very steep learning curve at the beginning I started feeling really good."

The conversation carried on easily, catching up with what was going on in each other's lives, their loves and all the things that friends share. Gina was the service centre manager when Sue joined Cuthbert's and quickly saw that she was smart enough and strong enough to work towards a management position. Kat, the new administrator, started on the same day as Sue and they very quickly became a successful triple act of manager, deputy and administrator. They all started by respecting each other and being willing to get things done. Gina dealt with the senior management and took responsibility for the department as a whole. Sue made sure the individual parts of it were able to do what was needed. Kat just magically made things happen so everyone else could get on with their jobs. Gina and Sue took great pride in making sure that existing staff got the training they needed, and new staff were only brought in when needed. They also became really good friends.

The whole place changed when the Teatherstone-Fox Group took over, and not, as far as Gina was concerned, for the better. While they were talking, Gina realised that her mind was wandering back to those days and she needed to stop thinking about it quickly for the sake of her enjoyment and her sanity.

"Let's get to our dinner reservation," Gina announced.

As it was her birthday Gina had decided to satisfy an old wish and go to a very high-style restaurant for dinner. She knew Sue's finances weren't up to it, but as soon as she knew that Sue was in London anyway on that day she managed to convince her to let the birthday girl pay for it. So her birthday included friendship and a great meal. Luckily for both of them, a new high-end restaurant had just opened in London's West End, run by a well-known chef, and it had had great reviews. It seemed to fit all Gina's requirements so that's where they went.

The meal was everything Gina had hoped for: wonderful food that looked beautiful, tasted just as incredible and wasn't fancy for the sake of it. Nothing was 'de-constructed' and there were no pointless 'emulsions' or poncy decorations, just great British food cooked and served according to vintage recipes. Sue had been afraid that the service would be stuffy but actually the waiting staff were very friendly and didn't look down on her or laugh when she asked what some of the words on the menu meant. One of the waiters didn't even seem to mind when Gina asked if he'd take their picture with her phone. She had a near pathological hatred of 'selfies' and he was good enough to make sure the picture had the rest of the restaurant in shot so that Gina had a photographic memory of a lovely evening. Then, of course, she inspected the photo to make sure they didn't have stupid-looking expressions on their faces.

"Well, that's how to ruin a perfectly brilliant evening." Gina suddenly looked as though she'd been shot. With no warning or explanation she slammed her phone onto the table and looked like she felt nothing but hatred.

"What's wrong?" Sue asked with concern and some confusion.

"Look at that!" Gina said, passing over her phone showing the picture the waiter had just taken. "So much for not mentioning them again."

Sue looked at the picture, and at first all she could see was her and Gina smiling in the foreground. It was only when she looked at the background that she could just about spot someone familiar getting ready to sit down at one of the tables further back.

"Isn't that…?"

"TF Junior, yes. The prize A1 arsehole who made my life a misery and the reason I left Cuthbert's."

Sue looked back at the picture to work out who he was with. She didn't think it was too surprising that TF himself was there, he had probably read the same review as Gina, but there was also the woman who had been at that day's meeting, and another man she didn't recognise.

"No! I am not going to let him do this to me again." Gina's mood had changed again, equally as strongly, showing absolute determination. "It's my birthday and I will enjoy it. I know a great comedy drag club. Let's go and have a laugh." So she signalled for the waiter to bring her the bill and they left with polite thanks and a determination to have a good time no matter what.

Barely a couple of months after the Teatherstone-Fox Group 'merged', Junior landed on the IT department and started trying to impose his designs on an already working system. He tried to convince people that he was 'one of them' and 'we're all geeks together' but nobody liked him. It was very obvious that he was the thirty-something son of a rich man who acted as though he had the God-given right to be where he was and be in charge of the minions. He clearly wasn't an idiot and knew his stuff about IT but he was absolutely no good at dealing with people.

He wasn't a bad-looking man but his demeanour instantly put any women off when he used that superior tone to try and ingratiate himself towards them. He had this way of looking and sounding as though he was taking the few women in IT just as seriously as the men, when actually he was being patronising and a bit creepy. 'Slimy' was a word often used. It wasn't an overt sliminess, nothing that could be reported as harassment, no stray hands or wandering eyes, but the women in the team were definitely treated differently. None of them were listened to properly, and it was obvious he didn't expect them to know as much about IT, although the attractive ones did seem to get more attention. It got even worse when he met the service centre team, and particularly Gina.

Because of the necessary overlap between IT and the service centre, TF Junior spent a lot of time with both. Gina had heard the rumours about him through Sue, and she went into the first meeting determined not to assume he was some kind of pantomime baddie, but she was saddened to discover that he actually lived up to every stereotype. He was still making all the right noises about 'Cuthbert's values' and treating everyone equally, but in reality he took firm charge. When it came to the interdepartmental meetings, his true intentions became clear. Gina was definitely on his radar. She was a tall, slender, attractive woman whose obvious intelligence was not what he regarded as of primary importance.

At first Gina didn't spot his intentions, then she ignored them, then she tried to make it just as obvious that she was not at all interested in anything more than a professional relationship. The problem, for both of them, was that he either failed to notice or chose to ignore her lack of interest. At a leaving dinner for one of Gina's staff, an occurrence that was starting to happen a little more frequently than it used to, TF Junior made sure he sat next to Gina and spent the entire evening trying to impress her with tales of his, admittedly young, achievements. On the rare occasions when she got a word in, she was as polite as necessary, and he was incredibly attentive in that way that made his intentions obvious. This was all mildly amusing, but at the end of the evening when he helped her with her coat he at least became honest.

"Look, it's obvious that we both like each other a lot. Why don't we go off for a drink together?" he said quietly, with a frighteningly conspiratorial tone.

Gina suddenly felt a little unclean and wanted to get out of there as quickly as possible. Obviously her manners, or his arrogance, meant he had completely misunderstood her feelings towards him.

"No, thank you," she said as firmly as her nerves could muster.

She was a strong independent woman but this suddenly made her feel vulnerable. She quickly went over to the colleague who was leaving, gave her a hug, wished her all the best and left the restaurant without another word. Sue spotted the disturbed look on her friend's face as she left but decided that Gina would ring over the weekend if something was wrong. There was no phone call, so Sue forgot about it.

Gina spent the weekend worrying about whether she had given off the wrong signals. By the time Monday started, when she had another meeting with him, she had decided that it was a simple misunderstanding and she would conduct the meeting on a purely professional level. At the meeting TF Junior acted as though nothing had happened, so everything seemed fine. Gina was relieved that maybe she didn't have to say anything.

After the meeting ended, Gina and TF Junior were the last people left in the room.

"I'm glad we have a chance to talk," TF Junior said with a worrying smile. "I should have realised that the other night was the end of a very long day and you were tired. Obviously we can schedule our drinks for a time that suits you better."

This level of arrogance took Gina by surprise; obviously he really could be that stupid, and it made her decision to reject him even more definite. Clearly this made it obvious that she needed to be a lot less ambiguous about her answer.

"Nicholas, I..." she started.

"Nick, please."

"It's obvious that you've got the wrong impression about me. Whilst I obviously respect you as a colleague," a clear lie, but Gina was confident his arrogance would allow him to assume that it was true, "my feelings do not go any further than that."

"Maybe for now, but I'm sure that after we've spent more time together your views will change."

Gina started thinking about the heavy club she was obviously going to need to get the message through to him. She tried to work out if it was true arrogance or some deep-seated compensation for a loveless childhood with a father obsessed by financial results. She managed to stop those thoughts quickly before there was any danger of something resembling sympathy.

"I am sorry, Nicholas, but I don't know how to put this more clearly. I have no interest in any kind of social relationship with you. I really don't want to appear rude but my answer will always be no."

"Fine," he answered, with a pathetic attempt to sound professional. "We'll say no more about it, then." And with that, TF Junior grabbed his papers and left the room in as businesslike and unaffected a manner as he could, while actually looking like a sulky schoolboy.

Nothing more was said for several weeks, which suited Gina fine; TF Junior was equally as businesslike with everyone. Then the real face of the Teatherstone-Fox Group was shown; all the branch managers got the same email:

To: All branch management
From: John Teatherstone-Fox
Subject: Invitation to future improvements
TEATHERSTONE-FOX GROUP – Synergy in business
As you are aware, Cuthbert's is undergoing some remodelling to bring it in line with other organisations within its new partnership. While the Teatherstone-Fox Group fully embraces the values that Cuthbert's has built its valuable reputation on, these changes will bring

out strong improvements in the operation, and hence success, of the company.

One of these changes is to bring consistency to the management structure. Within the next month all division managers will be invited to apply for their relevant positions within the new branch management structure. For the vast majority, this will be a formality and will allow all to ensure that they fit well within our family.

Regards

John Teatherstone-Fox

Teatherstone-Fox Group Director

A lot of blood drained from a lot of managers' faces as they quickly saw that they had to apply for their own jobs. For herself, Gina knew that she, with a lot of help from the rest of her team, had coped with all the recent changes incredibly well so she was shocked to discover that her well-written application had been turned down flat.

The letter from head office told her:

'We appreciate all your hard work and effort'

but

'on this occasion we have decided that a centrally based manager would fit better within our team.'

When she saw that she would be effectively demoted to deputy branch manager she knew exactly who was responsible. No specific head office manager had descended on the service department yet, so there had only been one such overlord who had seen her work. She stormed over to the IT department and into TF Junior's office to confront him.

"I'm very sorry that this decision had to be made. We all know that your team has done some good work, however we have to look at the big picture and consider who best works within our team."

The definition of 'we' was obvious to Gina but that wasn't her main issue.

"What do you mean 'some good work'? You wouldn't even have looked at us if my team hadn't worked so well with the rest of the company!" Gina felt her blood pressure getting higher by the second.

"Well, clearly you have a biased view on this."

"And you don't?" Gina knew what was really going on.

"Obviously you are not the kind of personality we can work with and you need to rethink your outlook."

"I need to rethink?!" Gina was seriously losing her normally calm manner. "You came onto me, remember, and don't think for a moment that I don't know why you are suddenly throwing your toys out of your pram."

By this point the entire office could hear exactly what was going on, and the already decreasing opinion of TF Junior descended a lot lower.

"Gina, really," he said in a voice that managed to be calming and patronising at the same time, with a recognisable tinge of creepiness, "I'm sure we can sort this out."

"No!" Gina said with barely contained anger. "You are right about one thing. There is no way I would ever want to work with you."

She stormed out of his office, went straight to her computer and started typing. Within five minutes her resignation letter was on his desk and she walked straight out of the building.

Changing the management titles to 'branch manager' sounded like a trivial thing but they started feeling the loss of control almost straight away. Sue felt it as much as anyone. She'd been a close assistant to Gina so it was no surprise when she got the fairly meaningless job of service branch manager. The small pay rise was the only compensation.

Even six months later Gina knew that she could never prove why she had been refused the job that should have been hers, but she knew the best revenge she could get was a successful life elsewhere and a bloody good birthday. She and Sue left the restaurant with absolute determination to enjoy that comedy drag club – which they did.

10

April – the next day

Sue couldn't quite work out why, but something made her feel like things were really not right. She made sure Gina passed on a copy of that photo when they eventually got up the next day. The club had been a great idea and they didn't get back to Gina's until the very small hours; she didn't feel great when she got the train back home. She was a bit surprised that she had the wherewithal to get the picture before she left, but somehow it just felt necessary.

"How was your trip?" Jeff asked when Sue got home.

"Boring, enjoyable, almost ruined, potentially very interesting and a brilliant laugh – in that order."

"You care to elaborate?" he asked as his wife slumped down onto the sofa next to him and gave him a kiss.

"Get me a large mug of strong tea and I'll tell you all about it."

Jeff, who instantly knew his wife had had a heavy night, kindly obliged. Once she was suitably caffeinated she told him all about her previous day, skipping over the boring meeting because Jeff had read that script already.

"Let's have a look at that picture," Jeff said once she was done.

He was a good spouse and had let her finish the whole story even though his interest was piqued partway through. Sue opened up their shared laptop and logged into her email to find the picture Gina had sent her.

"Surely he's not that stupid!" Jeff exclaimed as he looked at the expanded picture.

"What?" Sue tried to interpret the disbelieving look on her husband's face.

"Do you remember when I had to go down to headquarters a few months ago for that meeting with TF Junior and his dad about how they were promising they wouldn't outsource IT? You know, the one that sounded pretty much like the one you've just had?"

"How could I forget? I met you and Terry for dinner when you arrived back and he ranted for Britain."

"You may or may not know of a supposedly trivial change that came in when TF took over. Cuthbert's had used the same reliable, provably independent financial auditing company for decades. Well, TF sacked them and brought in his own auditor. Apparently a well-known, fully independent firm that would supposedly 'do a more thorough job' than the old guys. At the beginning of our meeting TF introduced us to the new accountant and gave us a lecture about being helpful and making sure the auditors got all the IT help they needed to do a thorough job. So much for independence. That man, who TF Senior and his son are laughing and being so chummy with at that restaurant you went to last night, is the accountant we were introduced to as the so-called impartial auditor."

"OK. So they are a bit chummier than they should be, but what's that got to do with stupidity?"

"I haven't really told you why I've been spending so much time looking at worky stuff."

"I just put it down to your innate love of all things techie."

"Yeah, well, if I'm honest that has got a bit to do with it, but I found out some stuff that seemed very interesting but didn't quite make sense, until now. Are you sitting comfortably? Then we'll begin."

Having quoted his favourite children's programme, Jeff explained all about the conversation with Terry and the history behind it, all the searching he had done through the software and that tiny little change buried where it shouldn't have been seen that meant that a significant chunk of money was being diverted out of company hands.

"How much money are we talking?" Sue's curiosity had been piqued but she still wasn't sure how this related to her trip.

"As far as I can see this is all of the direct debit money for the financial products. It's only part of the company's takings but still a very big wodge of money. The family was proud to announce last year that the financial products took over one and a half billion quid. I know we see those numbers bouncing around but suddenly it dawned on me just how much money that is. That works out as a cool 139 mill profit. I did a bit of rough calculation around how much of that is the direct debit stuff and I reckon we're easily talking around fifty mill that year. That means that TF Junior, and it turns out the rest of the clan, will pocket around four mill per month!"

"Nice," Sue responded. "Imagine what you could do with that as small change."

"What's more significant is *where* this was done. There is only one person who could have done this."

"Cue dramatic music," Sue interrupted with a cheeky grin.

"The thing is," Jeff continued with a matching grin, "this tiny little change was buried in a bit of the code that only I and TF Junior are supposed to be able to get to."

"You're very clever, dear, but, going back a bit, are you saying he made the change and is nicking the money?"

"That's exactly what I'm saying."

"So, not only is that man an immoral git for how he treated Gina but he's also a thief."

"Actually, Gina's photo proves that there's more to it. I found this out but I couldn't work out how he was getting away with it. The financial auditor would have spotted the missing money."

"And they changed the auditor for someone they turn out to be chummy with. Smooth."

"Bingo!" Jeff agreed. "And TF Senior being there strongly suggests they are all in on it."

"But why would they be so stupid to go somewhere where they could be seen and recognised?"

"It could be good old-fashioned arrogance. They probably assume only people like them can afford such a place. And don't forget it was pure fluke that you two were there and took that photo in that direction at that moment. Otherwise I'd have been left with a puzzle that made no sense."

"But why?" Sue asked.

"Why would it have been a puzzle?" Jeff asked back.

"No," Sue replied, looking a bit perplexed, "why is this rich kid doing this? The Teatherstone-Fox Group is big enough, and definitely ugly enough, to make plenty of money through legal means. Why is he bothering to steal extra money?"

"That is a very good question that worried me a bit too. I thought it might just be a rich brat trying to make a mark for himself but I did a bit of digging. The Teatherstone-Fox Group started out pretty small in the mid-'90s, buying another, much smaller financial company. The company grew a bit, profitability went up a bit. A year later they bought another, this time much bigger, company, which is a bit surprising because the profitability of the first company didn't go up by that much. They could have got a loan, I suppose, but the same pattern has kept repeating itself ever since. Occasionally they sold companies off but they never made enough to explain the next purchase. And never enough to persuade a bank that the profits were big enough to be sure of paying back a sizeable loan."

"Are you suggesting they've been pulling this scam every time?"

"I can't prove it but it fits the pattern. Maybe that's how TF Junior got to be a rich kid. There's another part to it that may do a better job of explaining the 'why'."

Sue sat still for a moment, staring at her cooling tea, trying to take it all in. Jeff gently took her mug and replenished both their drinks. More caffeine was going to be needed.

"Good old-fashioned tax evasion," he continued, as the cogs worked themselves out in Sue's very smart but very 'morning-after' head. "I've been looking it up and the auditor has to check things like the tax burden, so there must be a bit of 'careful accounting' to make sure things look OK for the taxman. They steal all this money, they've got a pet auditor who is good at pretending he didn't see the gaps, and they tell the taxman about the much smaller amount. They get all that money tax-free."

"Sorry," Sue said, looking puzzled, "my brain is trying to make sense of all this. Can we go back a bit? What happened before they started with all this? They must have come from somewhere, got the money for the first one somehow."

"That I don't know. The trail doesn't seem to exist before that first company was bought. They can't have come from nowhere but I couldn't work out where."

They both went quiet again, trying to work it all out.

"But there must be other, probably less illegal, ways of avoiding tax." Sue's mind skipped back to the subject before last. "There are always news reports about that sort of thing; suggestions of all sorts of multibillion-pound companies owing governments all sorts of money. Why else would they be messing about doing it this way?"

"That particular bit of the 'why' I can't help with. Force of habit, maybe? Maybe Junior found a trick and they just stuck with it. It's a relatively simple scam. Maybe it's easier than the alternatives. At the end of the day I haven't the foggiest. We may never know the answer to that question."

They went quiet again.

"So, what do we do now?" Sue finally broke the silence with the obvious question.

"Another very good question. I don't know why but somehow just reporting it to the police doesn't quite seem right yet. I don't know enough."

"True. I mean, you've got a good friend who used to be a policeman and who deals with computer-based fraud. Rob would be the right person to talk to about all this. But I agree we need to think about it a bit more before we do anything," Sue agreed, clearly deep in thought.

11

"He was right!" Jeff declared as he dropped his bag onto the dining table less than a month after their discovery. Sue thought she knew her husband entirely after nearly two and a half years together but she couldn't work out if the tone in his voice was that of anger, resignation, amusement or a weird combination of them all.

"You'll have to give me a bit more than that," she answered.

"I probably didn't mention it at the time, but when he left, Terry predicted the dreaded 'O' word everybody's been terrified of – outsourcing," Jeff continued.

"Not that I remember," Sue replied while handing him what seemed to be a well-needed beer.

"Thank you, I need that. After our discoveries I started keeping an eye on the business-level email traffic. Despite all their promises about people not losing their jobs, the wonderful Teatherstone-Fox Group today sent the financial department the following email."

He handed her a folded printout of an email he dug out of his back pocket.

To: Finance branch management

From: John Teatherstone-Fox

Subject: Cuthbert's future

TEATHERSTONE-FOX GROUP – Synergy in business
Having spent considerable effort bringing Cuthbert's
brand within the Teatherstone-Fox Group family and
thoroughly analysing the productivity of its various
components, we have come to the decision that there is
room for enhancing the performance and reducing the
outlay created in some areas.

Despite considerable effort on our part it has not
been possible to avoid significant changes. The first
area to receive these improvements will be the finance
department, where we will consider how external
resources can be used to maximise productivity. Branch
management is invited to attend a meeting, date tbc,
when the details will be discussed.

John Teatherstone-Fox

Teatherstone-Fox Group Director

"Discussed, my arse. We were right all along; they are
planning to outsource everyone they can! This is just the
start. Jobs will be lost. Expert knowledge of what good
service means will be lost. The whole thing will be given to
a bunch of people who will charge a fortune to do a useless
job and then another fortune to bodge a fix."

"So much for all the promises about keeping to
Cuthbert's philosophy."

"They've probably got an expensive bunch of lawyers
who have helped them define 'considerable effort' and
'possible' in any way that suits them. So, now they will

sell off real people's jobs to the lowest bidder and blame us when it doesn't work. That's exactly what Terry predicted and I was stupid enough not to believe him." Jeff's vitriol was so clear that the words were almost irrelevant. Sue could tell from the tone of his voice how angry he was when she scratched just below the surface. "They've started on this department and the rest will only be a matter of time."

He stopped and fumed, staring at the beer for a while before he carried on.

"We've had all that information about them for weeks now. It's about time we used it to give them what they deserve. I'm phoning Rob; he'll know who to pass this on to." Jeff held out his hand towards Sue so she could pass him the handset sitting beside her; he could then call his best mate. "We'll see whose jobs get lost when they are arrested for fraud or theft or whatever it's called."

"Hang on a sec," said Sue, holding the phone away from him. "I think you're looking at this the wrong way."

"They'll get what they deserve, the lying, thieving bastards!"

"Absolutely, but I've been thinking about it over the last few weeks and I reckon there's a better way."

"Better than seeing them slopping out in prison?" Jeff looked very unconvinced.

"Maybe. I've got two questions for you."

"I'm in no mood for riddles." Jeff's exasperation was starting to spill towards his wife, who just didn't seem to be getting it.

"Go with me, this may make sense, and if it doesn't we'll go back to your plan. First question. Given what we know about TF Junior's activities, would you agree that there is no way they are going to do this to the IT department anytime soon because he needs to keep control for his scam to work?"

"People are still going to lose their jobs!" Jeff said, showing his compassion.

"Yes, and they deserve to be punished for it. Second question. Do you have the skills to play them at their own game?"

"What are you on about?" He was getting tired with a mixture of anger and confusion.

"Actually, thinking about it, there's a third question. Do you have the morals to play them at their own game?"

Jeff looked at his wife in confusion... then slow dawning followed by disbelieving realisation. He was a smart man, and no matter how bad his day had been he still liked to think he knew her. She couldn't be thinking what he was starting to hear.

"Sorry, I'll be less cryptic. Maybe when I say this out loud it will sound really stupid and we'll go back to plan A." Sue knew she needed to stop messing around and just say what she meant. "You said that what he's done is actually really simple. Maybe that means you can do it as well. Maybe we can..."

"Are you actually suggesting that we become thieves ourselves?"

"Well, why not?!" she asked, more uncertainty coming through in her voice.

Jeff stared at her, wondering who the stranger sat next to him was. "I need a pee," he eventually said as he put his can down, very carefully planted his feet parallel to each other, stared at them for a few seconds and slowly got up.

Sue got up and poured herself a glass of wine. Given the small size of their flat she knew she could carry on talking to Jeff and he'd easily hear her, especially as he rarely closed the door. She also knew that her husband needed time to think so she went silently back to the sofa and sat back down.

Eventually the toilet flushed and Jeff came back into the room.

"I don't know what upsets me most, the thought itself or the fact that you had it. You know that I could have gone that way when I was younger but I worked damn hard to make sure I didn't have to. Now you're suggesting I make myself as bad as them. I thought we were good people."

His confusion and anger were now joined by a small amount of sorrow. The system Jeff went through as a kid hadn't been a bad one but he could have 'got in with a bad crowd', and he made sure he used his brains to avoid it.

"I'm sorry, darling. I never meant to insult you. Like I said, if it's stupid we'll turn them in." Sue reached for the phone and handed it to Jeff. "Rob's probably the right person. You ring him."

Jeff took the phone from her and dialled the number he knew off by heart. He still had a look on his face that gave away his feeling of disappointment. "It's engaged," he said as he hung up and put the handset down on the sofa arm. "I'll try again later."

Sue silently got up and made dinner, not daring to say anything. She felt like a total idiot for even starting the conversation. She should have known better, but in her head, before it was hampered by reality, it had seemed reasonable. She was not an openly teary person but she hated herself throughout the awkwardly silent dinner for having hurt the man she loved so much. Somehow, though, she knew enough not to make matters worse by trying to talk about it. Not yet anyway.

After dinner Jeff went into the spare room and left Sue on the sofa, hugging her knees and drinking more wine.

12

"I hate them too," Jeff said suddenly from the living room door without any warning, making Sue look up sharply, "but surely we're better than them."

"I know it was a stupid idea but I couldn't stop thinking that the best way of punishing them was to hit them where it hurts them most, their pockets. It was ridiculous. Please forget I said it."

"It's not that easy." Jeff took another beer from the fridge and sat back down next to Sue. He took a swig and stared at the can for a few seconds. "Particularly as you might have a point."

"Beg pardon?" Sue really was confused now. Had she upset him or not?

"It is a stupid idea but it might work. I could change the software in exactly the same way but divert the cash to us." Clearly, while Jeff had been in the spare room, some kind of switch had flicked in his brain and his moral concerns had been replaced by curiosity about the IT challenge.

"But what about your feelings about honesty? I don't get it."

Jeff opened his beer and took a swig. "The more I thought about it the more I realised that I don't have enough evidence to prove it's not me."

"What?"

"I have just as much access to that bit of software. We've both got rights to adapt it to Cuthbert's needs. TF Junior did all the work on it; he was very precious about being the one who made sure the external software fitted together with our stuff. I only had a cursory look at it at the time 'cos I had other things to worry about back then. It was only after that chat with Terry that I had a proper look and found what he was so precious about."

"So, you can't prove he was the one who did whatever was done?"

"It was such a tiny change, either of us could have done it at any time. We're both clever enough to have changed the logs to hide our tracks. I can't prove it was him!" He considered getting angry again but then drank some more beer and decided that staying rational was a better idea.

"The other problem is where the money's going. I did a bit of digging just now and the money goes to an organisation whose name means nothing to me. Could be anything – a company, a charity, anything. I did searches through Companies House and charity directories but couldn't find anything. From there, who knows where the money goes? I don't know much about business workings but I'm willing to bet there is some kind of clever trail that makes it almost impossible to trace the money back to the TFs."

"So much of this seems like supposition," Sue commented. "What can we actually prove?"

"Exactly. The auditor is someone they know, but that doesn't prove anything is being hidden. TF Junior is an arsehole but not even Gina could prove she was passed up for that job because she said no to him."

"If you were the one to report it to Rob wouldn't that count as proof it wasn't you? Or at least it's less likely to be you?"

"Maybe yes, maybe no, I'm not sure. But I am more and more sure that you were right in the first place. For what they are trying to do to our company and our friends they deserve to be hurt, badly, where it will hurt them the most. The legal way can't be relied on to do that. Your way can. "Congratulations, in thirty seconds you have managed to perfectly summarise what took me weeks to work out."

Sue didn't know whether to be affronted or amused. "It isn't quite that simple. We'll have to work out a lot of details to make sure the right people get hurt. Or at least to make sure that the people in the right don't get hurt."

*

Over the following two months Sue and Jeff discovered that it wasn't diverting the money that was the difficult bit. They quickly worked out that it was covering their tracks that they had to concentrate on. Being the organisational pedant that she was, Sue insisted that they start by sitting down and listing out what was needed, which turned out to be essential given how complicated it was going to be.

Sue's pedantry, or as she preferred to call it, common sense, went as far as to start out by writing down the many jobs on a single sheet of paper on a hard surface. She'd seen it on some old spy movie she'd watched on a rainy weekend afternoon as a way of making sure there was no evidence inadvertently left imprinted on the lower sheets in a pad.

They knew the computer they had was linked too much to Cuthbert's so they worked on paper until they could get a dedicated laptop. When they did, Jeff's security expertise would ensure future lists could not be hacked into by anyone without more computer power than currently existed on their planet. As with all sophisticated security systems, they both knew the weakest link could be the human factor, so they made sure their passwords were as random as possible and had nothing to do with them, Cuthbert's or their plans. Once they got it and set it up, the laptop could take over and they could burn the paper.

Some of their earlier planning was done with a little too much wine or beer in them, so a few of the early ideas were less sensible than they needed to be. They quickly worked out that the stakes for this project were so high they had better keep clear heads before making any decisions. A whole collection of silly code words was a prime example of such silliness.

They felt that the early notes made on paper were a weak link because they only had a lockable drawer in a desk pedestal, which could have easily been broken into. So they wrote in non-specific language that wouldn't give too much away. They wrote things like 'Prancer' (the reindeer partner to Dancer) for laptop and 'Baracus' (as in BA Baracus from *The A-Team*) for the bank account they would put the money into. Of course, the money itself was 'pasta sauce'.

The very first conversation they had using those words made them realise just how ridiculous they were and how much more suspicious things sounded with nonsense words. It was the following Friday night when the stresses of the week really built up for both of them, and the first bottle of wine was opened almost before they took their coats off. Sue was feeling particularly stressed and the first glass was finished before she'd changed out of her suit. Neither of them had eaten much that day so the wine hit empty stomachs, which is never a good idea.

Feeling the effects of the wine faster, Sue started the conversation about their plans first.

"So, let me make sure I've got this straight. Santa," their code for Nicholas Teatherstone-Fox, or Saint Nick as they ironically called him, "is moving his portion of the main pasta sauce into his Baracas before it goes into Bert's Baracas but after the supplier gets his pasta sauce put into his Baracas. So the supplier gets the expected right amount of sauce for them. Is that right?"

Jeff, who hadn't felt the effects of the booze quite as fast, practically spat his mouthful of wine out all over Sue.

"OK, first point of order. We are going to have to change that code. Anybody overhears that, it's going to sound like you're talking to the voices in your head or you've taken LSD. They'd probably phone the police just to get you sectioned."

"Point taken. It did make me want to giggle a bit," Sue said with a very daft grin on her face. "We'd probably better talk like grown-ups or they will put us away before we ever get the chance to do anything wrong."

They vowed to firstly, never use them again; and secondly, do all their planning sober. From that point on they never wrote any incriminating words where they could be found and never discussed it where they might be overheard. For the rest of the evening they limited themselves to eating dinner, watching a good film and talking general rubbish. For the first time in a while they started to feel like they were control of the pattern of their lives and were able to relax.

*

The relaxation had to be kept under control. They both knew just how risky the whole project was; they were under no illusions. If they got caught they would go to prison and the real baddies would probably get away with it. Neither of those things seemed good, but if they were truly honest with themselves, the thought of the TFs not getting what they deserved rankled more. Right from the outset they spent a considerable amount of time thinking about risk.

"How do we make sure TF Junior never finds out about our idea?" Sue asked during one of their many evening discussion sessions.

"Actually, that's easier than you'd think," Jeff answered. "He put his bit of code where he thought no-one would ever find it. I'll basically do the same. I know the systems better than he thinks I do. Of course, that's assuming his arrogance is as big as we think; so I'll make sure I use some old bits of software that existed before he got involved and which everyone has forgotten about. And I can keep a close eye on a very useful activity log which can give us warning if he starts looking anywhere dangerous. Of course, I can also keep an eye on the accounting reports to make sure they show what we know they should show."

"That reminds me…" Sue suddenly remembered a thought that had kept her awake a few nights before. "We'll work it out properly later, but we need to make sure that if things start going horribly wrong, if any of these risks look like they could happen, we will need to set things up so we can disappear, fast."

"Agreed."

"Another worry is what happens if he looks at his account and realises that it isn't as big as it should be? We can't just assume he won't want to crow over any trophies, or in fact spend it."

"Yeah, you're right, but there are several things on our side. He's only just started so he won't know how much should be there; everybody's still in a mess with the new accounting system so any changes will be easy to hide. Other than that, and most usefully, we are not as greedy as he is. I've been checking the sums and we can still do very nicely out of the deal if we only take part of it. Cuthbert's has made a lot out of this part of the business so we can afford not to be too greedy."

"How much you thinking?"

"I reckon if we keep it under a mill per month it won't be quite so noticeable. How does nine hundred a month sound? That's around a quarter of what they're taking."

By that point they'd become comfortable enough with it to not bother with the £1,000 multiplier, but they both agreed that that amount sounded very nice indeed. Nearly eleven mill per year sounded even nicer.

"He'll still be getting more than he deserves out of this. A part of the point was to punish those evil gits." Sue's anger was never far from the surface, even though her language did not match her true feelings.

"You'll get no disagreement from me, so how about this for a plan? We've agreed to set things up so we can disappear immediately if anything goes wrong, right?"

"Right."

"If all goes right we only take a bit at a time, as planned, for now and maybe one day we do disappear because we want to. I'm pretty sure I can set things up so that when we're ready we can take that whole month's lot, maybe even more, and disappear when we choose to with a shedload and really hurt him."

"I'm liking this more. I feel a bit of pride in the fact that I'm not geeky enough to know how you're going to do it, but as long as you're sure you can do it, I'm in."

*

The rest of the plan took a lot more work but if either Jeff or, more particularly, Sue were totally honest, they loved it. They used the classic line that it was the most fun either of them had ever had, certainly with their socks on. There were a few nights they didn't get as much sleep as they should, through planning or worrying, but the feeling of new-found control actually helped them rest better on most nights.

Sue's love of planning went into overdrive when they got the laptop and its security set up. There were charts showing each job, who was going to do it, how long it was likely to take, how it related to other jobs, sub-tasks making up each job and, of course, when they were going to be ready to start the scam. The laptop itself was set up with a separate internet router so the only traceable location was to the house and not to the laptop. They were always very careful to avoid doing anything through that router that would pique other people's interest and make them search for the IP address.

They had to work fast. Jeff developed his own very well hidden activity log that showed that TF Junior hadn't actually started, but they had to be ready when he did. This wasn't too much of a problem; Jeff knew exactly what he had to do.

It turned out to be the backstory that took more thinking about and preparation than they had realised.

"I've been thinking about where we are going to store our bit," Sue said. "I don't think we can just squirrel that amount away and hope nobody notices. If a life-changing amount suddenly turns up in our bank, they, not to mention the Inland Revenue, are going to start asking questions."

"You've obviously been giving the non-geeky side of this a lot of thought. Help me out here, how do we get round this?"

Sue continued, "Our bit needs to leave the company and not go anywhere near us. We know TF and co. are sending it to some disassociated account, probably offshore; why don't we do the same?"

"Go on."

"We need to find other people to take the stuff and invest it somewhere no-one will ever associate with us. People with lives that can never be traced to us. People we can trust implicitly."

"Brilliant idea. One tiny little detail. Where... how... do we find these people?" Jeff was feeling less and less like he knew what was going on.

"Easy," Sue responded with a very slight smugness and a little too much enjoyment for Jeff's liking. "Well, easy-ish," she conceded. "We become them!"

After that conversation, over the next few evenings Jennifer and Mark were invented. Sue and Jeff worked backwards, from the Swiss bank account they realised the money would have to go into, to the kind of people who would have such an account. It seemed obvious that Mark and Jennifer had to fit in to their environment and seem like they belonged there. Sue and Jeff even spent several hours picking their names from websites of common boys' and girls' names. They had to be nice names that rich people might have but not so notable they'd stand out in a crowd.

They had a very short conversation about where their alter egos should live. Shortly before, they'd both watched a travel show about Italy and instantly fell in love with the place. As things were, they couldn't afford to go, but suddenly they realised that fantasy could become reality; they didn't have to be bound by 'normal life' limitations. They started getting excited by the thought of internet shopping for mansions in Tuscany and flashy sports cars.

"Hang on a sec." Jeff leant back from the laptop, putting his hands behind his head. "We're getting ahead of ourselves. They can't even afford this yet. This is all beautiful but is it actually what they need, or want? Besides which, they're going to be rich but not 'mansion' rich."

Some of the conversations had gone like that; mostly both of them were really sensible but occasionally one of them got a bit over-excited and needed to be reined back in. After a bit of thought they decided that Jennifer and Mark would want to live in a city in northern Italy, so they could get to the Swiss bank if necessary and enjoy the lifestyle. A quick bit of internet digging showed some very nice apartments in the middle of Milan that actually suited them better than quiet mansion life. They knew they couldn't do anything until they had taken the first few instalments. That money would have to start off being held in a UK account and later be transferred to the reputable but not too big Swiss bank they found when there was enough of it. It really did feel good to know what the eventual goal was.

13

Late May

"Friends!" Sue suddenly called out into the darkness, sitting bolt upright in bed a few nights later.

"Wassup?" Jeff slurred in sleepy confusion as he turned the bedside light on and reached towards his wife. She was sitting there staring somewhere into the distance.

"How can we just leave our friends?"

Jeff wiped his eyes and desperately tried to make sense of what he was suddenly confronted with. After what seemed an age, all the bits and connections slotted together in his mind.

"All this was your idea, remember? Why are you suddenly stressing about it at... oh my god," Jeff's face scrunched up as he looked at the clock, "seventeen minutes past three in the morning?"

Sue turned and looked blankly at Jeff. Then, with just as little warning as her original outburst, she lay down and fell back to sleep. Jeff swore again, turned the light off and, after he'd managed to calm his mind down, eventually got back to sleep himself.

Neither of them functioned very well at work the next day. Sue only had a vague memory of something being not quite right. When Jeff cooked dinner that evening Sue spent the time silently staring at the table, and then at the food Jeff placed in front of her. Finally he got fed up of waiting and asked:

"Are you going to tell me what last night was all about?"

Sue looked a bit confused. "How d'ya mean?"

"Um, your sudden outburst at three seventeen, remember?" he responded, equally confused and put out by her confusion. "Something about our friends."

Suddenly it all came back and Sue just felt annoyed with herself for forgetting.

"I'm sorry, love, I half woke up and my mind started half dreaming about all our plans. I think it started positive enough, you know, vague thoughts of us swanning around Italy, but suddenly I started thinking about Kat and Rob. They're our best friends. We've known them for years and we're planning to lie to them and eventually just disappear. We're supposed to be decent people." She looked like she was going through major worries in her head. "Good people don't do that to their friends. Do they?" she asked, looking almost plaintively at Jeff.

Jeff took a swig of his beer and thought for a minute.

"Yeah, after your alarm call this morning I lay there for a bit asking the same question."

"This seemed like such a good idea to start with and suddenly I'm not sure. TF and co. deserve it but are we giving up more than it's worth? And yes, I know this was all my idea in the first place but, well, all the 'buts' suddenly started spinning through my head. Strangely it's not the thievery bit that made me question whether I could still call myself a good person," Sue continued. "We can happily believe we have no choice about that, but good friends don't just disappear. Do they?" The normally strong-minded Sue suddenly felt she needed confirmation of what she'd always thought to be obvious. The very definition of good and bad seemed questionable.

Jeff sighed. At three nineteen that morning, once he'd worked out what was going on, much the same questions started going through his mind, and he'd been distracted by them all day. His thoughts were complicated by his own history and how he'd spent years striving to redefine himself, as Sue put it, as a decent person.

"I know exactly where you're coming from," Jeff finally said. "I thought I'd learned what good and bad people were years ago but it's not that simple." As Jeff had had all day to think about Sue's outburst, as opposed to her feeling not quite right but not remembering why, his thoughts were a little further on than hers. "A wise person once said to me that only saints and murdering dictators are truly good or bad. Everyone else muddles along in the middle somewhere, making compromises. I reckon, on balance, we've turned out OK. And at least we're better than 'them'." He made it obvious that 'them' were the true villains of the piece.

"I guess it's that balance thing I'm struggling with. I just don't want to be guilty of what so many politicians seem to do, and misdirect people's thoughts away from one thing being wrong by concentrating on something else that's wrong. Both things are still wrong," Sue replied. "Am I overthinking this?"

"No. These are good questions well asked, certainly better now that it's not the middle of the night. We need to be sure we're fully committed to this before we start. We both need to be OK with who we are. Personally, I think you're a great person."

"You're biased, but sweet." Sue felt a bit better about her place in the world. "I guess if we can work out a way of not hurting the people we care about I'll be a lot happier."

"Yeah, I've been thinking about that."

The conversation carried on for a while longer, going around in the same circles, where they swung from a determination to get TF no matter what the side effects were, to compassion for their great friends and a fear of becoming just the kind of people they were trying to punish. It had been such a good plan but the downside seemed impossible to ignore.

They took a break from the conversation to finally concentrate on the nearly cold dinner that had sat on the table, only occasionally getting nibbled at, while they'd been trying to answer the fundamental questions. When they were done they left the dirty dishes and went over to the sofa with more wine and beer.

"I've thought of a possible compromise. It might actually make everything a lot neater," Jeff said as they sat down.

"If you can think of a way of still having our cake and being decent people, I'm all ears," Sue replied.

"If our plan works, one day we are going to sweep up everything we can and disappear, right?"

"That's the plan."

"Then, what happens to TF and co., apart from getting less rich than they planned?"

"That sounds like more questions than answers," Sue said, the doubts starting to get stronger in her mind again.

"They might even call the police."

"Yes, that's not making me feel any better."

"Or worse, we don't know who else they know. It might get nasty."

"Will you please get to the bit that makes me feel better?" Sue was only getting more exasperated.

"What if we beat them to it even more? My oldest and best friend is a man who investigates just this sort of crime, right?"

Sue gave up answering and just did a kind of sideways nod in agreement, with a bit of raised eyebrow for effect.

"Who has good contacts with the relevant police department, right?" Jeff continued. "Instead of waiting for the bastards to find out and get this investigated themselves, we could amass enough evidence against TF and co. and make sure Rob gets it as we go."

"So he, and by association Kat, will hate us. Great!"

"I've thought of that too…"

The conversation carried on and, eventually, with a few details debated and eventually added, they both felt the original plan still worked and they could still sleep at night. The question was still there in both their heads but their mitigating plans made them feel better about themselves.

*

Jennifer and Mark quite easily became heirs to a regular income. They were going to need paperwork to prove their identities, which turned out to be easier to achieve than Sue had considered.

It turned out that while Jeff had indeed made sure he didn't fall in with the wrong crowd, he still knew what they could do and how to contact them. Sue didn't ask too many questions when Jeff disappeared one day with photos they had taken in their smartest clothes and hair. He came back without any explanation, but also without the savings he had taken that morning. Extra money was needed since biometric passports came into use. The contact of a contact of a contact who knew how to create the electronic chip with their faces on it, with all of the expected e-security, did not do his stuff cheaply.

A few days later Jeff disappeared again and returned with a pair of new passports in Jennifer and Mark's names, along with suitably filled in birth certificates. Jeff knew there was always a chance that the forger could give his identity away, but they had no way of knowing why he'd come to them and were hardly going to drop themselves in it by grassing up Jeff. Suddenly the alter egos became real people with provable identities.

*

The day everything was ready arrived. For all intents and purposes, Mark and Jennifer had become real people. In a rare idle gap in proceedings, Sue had even done a bit of internet-based window shopping at Harrods to decide what Jennifer would wear. They'd opened the UK-based bank account in Jennifer and Mark's names to accept the first few instalments until they had enough to transfer to Switzerland. They had even identified the small but well respected Swiss bank that would eventually hold Jennifer and Mark's 'inheritance money'. A bit later on, once they had established the account and visited the bank, they opened a safe deposit box and regularly left copies of the various bits of evidence against the Teatherstone-Fox Group in it, as backup.

Crucially, Jeff had everything in place to start shifting money away from TF Junior.

Not only did they have to invent a history for their alter egos that would explain the influx of money, they had to also come up with a convincing reason for occasionally disappearing to Italy without anyone guessing what was really going on. Sue had never talked to anyone about her parents. When she started at Cuthbert's it was still quite painful and she hadn't even told Kat that much. That there was a car accident was all Kat knew, and the point had never been taken any further. Even at their wedding the absence of parents had just been accepted.

Her parents had been very moral people and brought Sue up to strongly believe in justice. They would definitely have approved of making sure the Teatherstone-Fox Group got its comeuppance. So the other character who got invented, or rather re-invented, was Sue's mum, who had not been killed in the car accident, but lived in a Welsh care home and regularly needed visiting.

To get this information where it needed to be, Sue made sure the next day was a 'particularly bad day'. Actually it was no worse than normal at a time when none of them were that good. After a quick, tired-looking word with Kat, they agreed to meet up at a local pub that evening for a much-needed drink. They both had work the next morning but were caring less and less, so Kat was only a little surprised when Sue seemed to be getting drunk faster than normal. Fatigue can do that.

The conversation eventually wandered around to their pasts.

"I've never told you much about my family, have I?" Sue suddenly slipped in between gulps of wine.

"There was a car accident, I know that bit, but the rest was up to you to fill in... if you ever wanted to," Kat answered.

"I was just thinking about my mummy," Sue said with a slightly drunk lilted tone to her voice, losing control more than Kat had ever seen.

"You've never mentioned her before. I'd always assumed she died in that accident."

"I guess she kind of did. She was so devastated when Dad was killed by that unthinking arsehole lorry driver." Sue suddenly found she didn't have to pretend she was feeling the anger and bitterness. Be it truth or only half truth, it was all still there, and it didn't take very much digging to unbury it. There had been a lorry driver, there had been a crash, there had been death and a great deal of pain, but Sue knew she had to bring her real feelings back into line in order to finish her task.

Getting her feelings sorted, Sue recounted the half true tale of her father being killed in that crash and her mother being so devastated that she lost her mind. Something had recently got worse and she needed to live in a care home. Sue had found a very nice one in a pretty part of north Wales, a reasonable drive away so she and Jeff could visit regularly. Sue still felt rough lying to such a good friend, and she kept having to remind herself that it would work out in the end. She hoped. The next time they saw each other Sue mentioned this, with far less emotion, to Francesca, to allow for future excuses.

The last thing Sue and Jeff did before the plan went fully active was take a nice Saturday morning drive to the nearest part of Wales, find a nice local bakery and buy its entire stock of Welsh cakes. They then went to a local pub for lunch and waited for another batch of cakes to be made, which they then also bought. They even bought as many unused plain paper bags as possible and put them straight in the freezer when they got home.

A pleasant drive to Wales every couple of years to find a different bakery and replenish the stock of 'holiday treats' was a small price to pay for their new life.

The morning came and went and absolutely nothing happened. The only thing that did go up was Sue and Jeff's level of paranoia. They both knew that so much was at stake they were reluctant to press the metaphorical start button. They checked and rechecked that everything really was in place, had one or two more angst-ridden conversations, knowing that once they started they could never go back, but they knew just how much they hated TF Junior, and if they were going to do it it had to be when he wouldn't notice the change. As soon as he started his scam he unknowingly started to change their lives forever. That evening, when they were sure it was all in place, Jeff pressed the right buttons and it began.

14

The following July

Jennifer and Mark had lived a good life, regularly visiting Milan for the last year. They easily made friends with their neighbours, who were about the same age and were descended from the mansion-style life they had originally wanted. They wondered whether to start getting known by other people there was really a good idea, but they decided there were two very good reasons why they should. Being well known as the silent couple who never talked to anyone went against their plan to fit in, so getting on with people was better. Also, they just weren't the silent kind of people. They liked people... well, most people, and part of their definition of this happy alter-ego lifestyle had to include people.

They easily invented lifestyles and careers that meant they had an excuse for only being in Milan for short times, Jennifer with her antiques and Mark with his family's old financial company, which he'd dragged into the IT era. They deliberately chose imaginary careers that sounded plausible but couldn't be too easily verified by anyone who was unhelpfully nosy. Jennifer came from a very wealthy family and had decided to keep her brain busy by running a boutique-style antiques business. This gave her a chance to indulge in what quickly became a passion for learning about, and occasionally buying, antiques. Jeff even built her a fake website with pictures of a mixture of English and Italian antiques. They were valuable but nothing was rare enough to pique a collector's curiosity.

Mark's family conveniently operated in very high-level international finance, which had nothing to do with ordinary people's, even moderately rich ordinary people's, lives. Jeff spent an incredibly boring day, before they got the Milan place, learning enough about that world to get by in a conversation if he really had to. Luckily it never came up, and even if it did he was ready with a client confidentiality excuse that meant he couldn't talk about it too much. And there was always the classic 'I'm on holiday and I don't want to talk about it' excuse.

Sue and Jeff got so astute at living their part of the lie that it became part of normal life. A year in, they decided to upgrade from the flat and buy a nice little terraced house. Nothing too ostentatious and no more than a couple of professionals like them could afford. Of course, even though they could afford it outright they got the mortgage everyone would have expected. They certainly had no qualms about eventually disappearing on the mortgage provider and letting them sell the place. They also didn't see why they shouldn't have a more comfortable life, albeit sensibly comfortable. On two incomes, with no kids, maybe they could have done better but they were able to explain a relatively modest house and lifestyle through the need to look after Sue's mum.

They bought their classic, terraced, two-storey house, once a working-class factory-tied house, which, as so often done these days, had been gentrified and inhabited by professional types. It must have been built for slightly higher ranks in the factory workforce because it had a front porch with a stylishly tiled step, which led to a narrow corridor. The living room door came off the side of the corridor and it eventually got decorated with some much-loved scenery posters. The corridor quickly led straight to the dining room, with the small kitchen at the back. This room layout suited them better than the terraced houses where the front door opened straight into the front room because they could furnish it more to their tastes. More importantly for Sue, there was more room upstairs so Jeff could have his own room in which he could do his computery stuff without bothering her.

They even managed to find one which still had some of the original features, like early 20th-century tiles and cast-iron work around the fireplaces. Sue particularly fell in love with the decorative and brightly coloured period tiles that went around the fireplaces. The simple but elegant designs showed that this was still a factory worker's house. The use of better than necessary design and its place in society interested Sue.

A simple passageway ran between their house and next door and led to a nice little backyard and the back door into the kitchen. In classic style this had been added as an extension sometime after it was built. The yard meant they could grow a few vegetables and herbs under glass, which suited their expanding tastes. Importantly it didn't need too much maintenance, which suited their lifestyle of frequent absences.

They were mostly very good at separating the two worlds – with only one incident of weakness. On maybe Mark and Jennifer's fifth trip to Milan, they saw a stunning 17th-century Italian glass decanter and goblet-style glass set that they both fell in love with. Over the years they had seen tacky reproductions of that sort of thing but this was the real deal. They were all made in a wonderful deep cobalt blue with gold inlays and looked so lovely. Whenever they drank out of them they were almost mesmerised by the effect of light through the glass and the glint of the gold. Very soon they realised they couldn't bear to be away from them so they took the set back home to England, to use as Sue and Jeff. They knew it was risky and breaking all their own rules but it was so gorgeous that they couldn't bear to only see it occasionally. Despite its age, considerable value and delicacy, they were able to convince Rob and Kat that it was just pretty tat that they happened to like.

They only used it for special occasions and the tat assertion became a running joke between them. So much so that they had to hide their tears when a very drunk Rob decided to help them after several bottles of wine and smashed one of the glasses while washing up. After that the set stayed in a glass-fronted cupboard and never got used again.

*

Over the next year several other departments, or at least major functions within departments, were outsourced in one form or another with no benefit to anyone except the TF Group's profit line. More people lost their jobs, or were re-employed as contractors, and Sue and Jeff only became more determined. Of course, IT would have been an early choice for the 'O' word but only Sue and Jeff knew that TF Junior's need to keep his scam in-house was the real 'why' behind why that didn't happen, and they were in no hurry to spread the news.

A support group started to help those made redundant, or those who had had enough of the loss of decent terms to find better jobs. Specialist employment agencies made sure people got what they *wanted*, not just what they needed. It meant some ex-employees were able to completely change their career paths in ways they never could have afforded before. In the meantime help was available to make sure everyone got any unemployment benefits they were entitled to, although nobody stayed on them for long. There was even independent legal advice so everyone got the redundancy pay they were due.

Everyone who used the services got the chance to keep in touch with old colleagues and friends, or they got a clean break if that was what they wanted. Nobody really questioned how all this was paid for once it was made very clear that the help was free and had no links to the TF Group. Mark and Jennifer waited a while before upgrading their Alfa Romeo, and Armani didn't do quite as well as it might have for a few months.

PART III

WHEN?

Present Day

15

December – Saturday evening

"Your boss is a pompous arse," Rob announced when he and Kat were over for a pizza and booze dinner that evening.

"Um… yes, we know. Have you only just worked this out from all our rants about them?" Jeff responded, looking a little puzzled by Rob's sudden statement.

"I had the – and I use the term loosely – 'joy' of meeting him this week."

Sue and Jeff couldn't look at each other. In a split second they both knew their world, their dreams and their very carefully laid plans might just have fallen apart and the back-up plan was going to have to be used. Still in that split second they both remembered where the emergency exit bags and paperwork were kept and how they would get to them. They knew this day might come but it had never occurred to them that it would come from Jeff's best friend.

Sue was about to try and nonchalantly enquire further but she was scared her voice would give away far too much interest in Rob's business. Luckily Rob had barely noticed the passing of that split second and carried on talking before any give-away questions were necessary.

"I suppose it's the curse of being a computer fraud investigator. The people you meet are rarely the people you'd choose to meet."

"What's up with our beloved TF?" Sue asked, hoping she had had enough time to control her voice.

"He's convinced he's being robbed, what else? He says that one of the businesses in his group, by which of course he means him, is getting a lot less money than it should be from some of its computer-based products. It's amazing how obvious it can be when people like him say all the right things about concern for the company and can still be so readably self-interested."

"It's like we've always said. Words are meaningless with him," Jeff finally answered, just about getting his head straight.

"Yeah, well, he was full of words, none of which made him sound like he knew what he was talking about. He went on and on about not being able to trust his employees and how he needed me to find the problem in the middle of the – and I quote – 'geeky ramblings'."

"I thought these things were normally related to cybercrime and all that," Sue added.

"Yeah, often, but he seems convinced this is something internal. I just do what I get paid to do," Rob responded.

"Is this something we should all be worried about?" Sue asked.

"I shouldn't really say too much, it being an ongoing investigation an' all, but I don't think it's big enough to put the whole company in danger. It's not even clear which part of his empire is the source of the problem. The thing is I could do with your help," Rob answered with a plea to his fellow IT expert. "My investigation will be a lot quicker if someone with full knowledge of one of the IT systems would show me round."

"I'll do my best, but are you sure I'll know the relevant bits?" Jeff replied, in some hope that however fake his modesty might sound, it might deflect from the turmoil in his head that he feared was visible.

"Maybe not, but it's a good place to start. They seem convinced the problem is coming from within the company rather than some clever kind of cybercrime, so that's where I need to look."

"Look," Kat interjected, "if you two are going off into geek-land, Sue and I will start on the service centre until you fall asleep. Surely there must be other non-work stuff we can all talk about."

Jeff and Sue desperately wanted to know more but they knew that pushing it further would look out of place. It would drive them nuts but they just had to wait and appear as unconcerned as possible while the evening descended into its usual beer-and-wine-fuelled laughter. They were careful about how much they drank. They both, still without any verbal communication, knew that control was more important than ever, which was a non-trivial exercise when they were trying to act naturally.

They didn't get much sleep that night. They talked around their new knowledge for a while, debating whether they should just cut and run or hang on and check whether they were in any danger, but they quite quickly realised that they simply didn't know enough to make a snap decision.

Unfortunately this didn't stop either of them worrying, and their busy minds made sleep hard to come by.

*

Sunday evening

They spent the next day doing lots of menial tasks aimed at keeping their minds off what was really worrying them. The house hadn't been that clean in a long time. That evening Jeff got the phone call he both desperately needed and dreaded in roughly equal measure. Rob still wasn't sure which part of the Teatherstone-Fox Group was being scammed but he wanted to learn how the system linked together, and of course check that the problem wasn't in Cuthbert's part. They arranged for Rob to visit the next day. The more Sue thought about it the more nervous she got.

"Why are we still here?!" Sue demanded that night over dinner. "We set up all these plans so we could disappear the instant things looked dangerous. Explain to me please why we aren't using them."

"There's a good chance this has nothing to do with us."

"You've been saying that since last night and I still don't buy it. I refer the honourable gentleman to my earlier question. Why, on this sweet earth, my darling love, ARE WE STILL HERE?!"

All the way through, Sue and Jeff had taken fairly equal turns to get nervous; Sue didn't really care if it was her turn or not. She didn't understand why Jeff didn't seem to be taking the threat to their plans, not to mention their liberty, seriously.

"I've been thinking about it," Jeff answered, "and I'm pretty sure I can make this work for us."

"'Pretty sure'? 'PRETTY SURE'?! I'm sorry, but given everything that's at stake I'm not settling for anything less than a 100% cast-iron, nailed-on dead cert. And then I want your blood if it goes wrong." She had been trying very hard to keep her stress and volume levels under control but it was getting harder and harder.

"Trust m…"

"Do NOT do that!" Sue's anger was barely hidden by that point. "DO NOT expect me to go along with a decision without evidence to back it up."

Throughout the whole scam they had always discussed every point, to make sure the risks were reduced as far as possible, and now, when it seemed to Sue to be the most dangerous situation they'd faced, Jeff appeared to be taking the biggest risk of all.

"I know the risks, but bear with me, I think the results will be worth it. Think of it this way: whether we like it or not, after all these years we still can't be sure that TF and family will get what they deserve. OK, we get to swan off with lots of money…"

"And our freedom," Sue interjected, justifiably, she felt, given the stakes.

"Yes, that too, but the other part of the deal was to drop those bastards well and truly in it. This could be our way of making very sure it happens. Rob needs me to show him around and I know I've done a good enough job of hiding our bit of the transaction to make sure he only sees TF's bit. And you may remember we want to make sure he doesn't think I started the whole thing."

"You've gone from 'pretty sure' to 'know'. How convinced are you, really?"

"The more I think about it the better I feel." Jeff was becoming more sure in his own mind as he thought through the things he'd have to do to make his idea work. "OK, how about this for a deal? Give me two days of conversations with Rob. If at any point I think he's going in the wrong – or from his point of view, right – direction I'll pull the plug and we'll go."

"Do you swear to me that you will stop the instant things look bad for us? You won't get too cocky?"

Sue knew her husband well enough not to worry about greed. Over the scam-filled years they had done well enough to fulfil their dreams and they both knew it. But right now it seemed like his ego needed restraining a bit.

"Promise. Like I said, trust me."

"Hhhmmm…" Sue's paranoia, again justifiable in her view, meant she might trust the man she loved very much but she would also keep a very close eye on him.

16

As arranged, Rob turned up at Jeff's department the next morning and the two of them sat down at one of the general computers in a side room, nice and privately, at TF's instruction. Rob was used to keeping his clients' worries quiet. It made sense that when bosses didn't know who was scamming them they kept the business quiet, but it was also clear that TF regarded the branch staff as being beneath corporate business.

Once the pre-requisite teas were made they got down to work. Their natural relaxed way with each other soon gave way to business as there was IT to be talked about. Both being equally IT literate, Jeff and Rob knew how to talk the same language, and Rob was quickly shown around the various parts of the IT system and how they interacted and fed information back to the Teatherstone-Fox Group system.

Being there to investigate fraud, Rob wasn't particularly interested in things like the service centre or warehousing parts of the system, and he steered the conversation more towards the parts that involved money transactions. From his own past experience, he wasn't at all surprised by how the whole system worked. Helpfully, Jeff had been very careful over the years to make sure the documentation showed exactly what was going on, so it was very easy to follow for someone like Rob, who knew his stuff. Jeff didn't even have to use his favourite pasta analogy.

Jeff and Rob still spent most of the day poring over the various bits of code, breaking only for lunch and the regular supply of tea. All the while, Jeff made sure that Rob stayed away from the incriminating parts of the code, made easier by the fact that TF Senior clearly had no idea what TF Junior had done and hadn't given Rob any specific directions.

*

Monday – 7.03pm

"Look, I don't want to be one of those wives who nag their husbands the moment they get in from work," Sue said, desperately trying not to sound exactly like that, "but I'm still not convinced we should still be here."

She knew that arguing wasn't going to help anything – they had always talked things through rationally – but her patience was running thin.

While Jeff was spending the day with Rob, Sue spent hers feeling like she was being silently tortured at her own office. There was no news from her husband about how things were going, so she had to endure the day in her own department dealing with Francesca's anger at her disappearance the previous week, without any hints at the turmoil going through her head. There were of course myriad little things she had to deal with to do with the day-to-day running of the service centre, for which she was actually grateful. The last thing she needed was a boring day which would allow her time to let her mind wander onto all the things that could possibly go wrong.

It was only once they'd driven home, which she did, again to keep her mind busy, that she felt able to discuss what was, or was not, going on. Jeff was even getting the dinner ready before Sue made her comment.

"Truly, my love, I know what I'm doing. I know he's a smart man but I can make sure he sees what we want him to. Besides which, this'll help me lead him towards TF and co. being the perpetrators."

"That's fine, but remember the whole bit about them not knowing it's us? How do you plan to avoid that?"

"I've made sure the changed code is in a bit he can't know about, let alone see, unless I show him. Junior himself doesn't even know about that routine. It'll be fine. Don't you worry your pretty little head about it." He should have known that even mock patronising-ness, which he felt sure Sue would know this was, was a very bad idea when things were so dangerous.

"Oh, go..." Sue started to tell her husband exactly what she thought of his reply, when the pasta they were having for dinner started to boil over.

"Your favourite pasta analogy boiling over – how pertinent," Sue remarked sharply as she turned the hob off.

She started to drain the pasta but her stress was starting to show through and she was shaking as she lifted the boiling water-filled pot.

Jeff took over from her, realising, far later than she had wanted him to, that this was no longer funny. Once he had poured the pasta into the metal colander waiting in the sink, he looked back at Sue and realised she was nearly in tears. She wasn't one of those people who cried with romantic-looking tears; her eyes went red and puffy, and anyone who really knew her, particularly her husband, realised that she was on the edge of a real breakdown.

Jeff quickly poured the pasta back into its dry pot to stay warm and went to cuddle his wife.

"I'm sorry," he said. "I know it's the wrong time for being daft, but give me until tomorrow, please, and then we'll decide what to do. I really do know what I'm doing, promise."

Sue still felt nervous but she trusted her husband enough to know he wouldn't take silly risks, and the hug did make her feel better. She would always keep her eyes open, checking for undue complacency or arrogance, but for now things seemed OK.

Maybe they were both equally nervous, but the sudden ring on the doorbell made Jeff jump as much out of his skin as Sue.

*

"Terry! What on earth…?" Jeff gasped as he opened the door. The nearby street light had blown and still hadn't been fixed by the council so the only light falling on the visitor came from the hall light inside. He almost didn't recognise the old colleague he hadn't seen since they went to their separate buses all those years ago. The reminder of a very different time only just stood on the doorstep looking like he was about to collapse.

"I guess you must have followed the money," Terry croaked as he looked up at Jeff through a very blackened eye and wiped his bloody nose with the back of his hand, leaning hard against the porch wall.

Jeff immediately stepped out to catch Terry as he looked like he was incapable of staying upright. Terry winced as Jeff put Terry's loose arm around his shoulders and held on around Terry's ribs. Jeff half supported and half carried him through to the dining room and towards the nearest chair.

"What the...?" Sue questioned as she finally saw who was being brought in with so much noisy fuss. Her sentence was stopped as she realised there were problems to deal with rather than swear at.

As Jeff carried on helping Terry sit down she went back into the kitchen, wet down some kitchen towel and then brought it and some dry towel over to join them at the table. As soon as Terry was as comfortable as he was going to be, Sue pulled another chair up close to him and started cleaning his very bloody and swollen face as gently as she possibly could. Every touch against the bruises made him wince even more, so her touch never seemed gentle enough.

"Mate, what the hell happened?" Jeff wanted to know why his old colleague had come to them in this state while quoting an old suggestion that had started his life changing.

"I could make a joke about 'you should see the other guy' but I'm really not in the mood." Terry sounded like talking was a lot of work. With some difficulty he lifted his arm to pull Sue's away from his face. "Leave it for now,

Sue, please. I mean, thank you, sweetheart, but I really just want to be still for a few minutes." Even breathing looked difficult.

"Of course. Is there anything we can get you?" While Jeff seemed to want answers, something in Sue just wanted to make things better.

"No, thanks. Just stillness sounds good. Besides, I don't fancy trying to drink through these lips, if they look anything like they feel."

Sue hadn't heard the money comment at the door so her concerns were just about helping a nice man. However, the next five minutes, when Terry just sat there with his eyes closed, not saying or doing anything, were torture for Jeff. He knew he had to be patient but he so desperately wanted to know more. All he could do was sit there and watch Terry breathe, shallowly, wheezily and with obvious discomfort. Despite Terry's refusal, he still got up to put the kettle on for the 'solves everything' cups of tea, even though he knew whatever had happened wouldn't be solved that way. He had to do something.

Eventually Terry opened his eyes.

"Make that a strong one for me," he said, vaguely nodding in Jeff's direction. He then weakly nodded at Sue, indicating that she could start her cleaning again. "I don't suppose you've got any frozen peas?" he asked as she was finishing. "My chest hurts."

As Jeff was about to bring over three teas, including the requested strong one, he stopped to look in the freezer for the peas and then brought everything over to the table on a tray. Terry took the peas and put them under his bloody shirt onto the side of his chest. He held them in place with one hand and used his other to pick up the tea. He quickly realised that, in a clearly weakened state, he needed both hands to deal with the tea. He lifted both of his hands towards the mug, which meant the bag of peas dropped out of his shirt. Sue picked it up and held it in place.

"Thanks," he said. "I guess drinking tea, holding that in place and breathing was getting to be too much."

Another five minutes went by with very little said. Terry just tried to concentrate on getting the tea first to his lips and then past his swollen, tender lips so he didn't dribble too much of it down his shirt. He wasn't bothered about looks, he just desperately needed to drink the tea.

Finally Jeff couldn't take any more. "How... I mean, why... I mean, what happened?" he asked, trying to keep his voice calm and not sound too demanding.

"Good questions, all. I think the what is pretty obvious – I got beat up," Terry answered, showing that the sarcastic sense of humour he had been very well known for would not be suppressed, no matter what. "How? This has never happened to me before but I think it was probably the usual way. There were fists and feet; I can't remember the details. Why? There's an interesting question. And you forgot the 'who', but I don't know that anyway."

Terry took some more tea to steal himself, ready for more explanation.

"Hang on a sec," Sue interjected. "Shouldn't we be getting you to a hospital? We don't know how badly you're hurt."

"It's OK," Terry answered. "My rugby days taught me what a busted rib feels like when it happens, and I just need painkillers and rest for that. Besides which, Jeff is doing his best but he's going to pop a cork if I don't explain my earlier comment."

Sue looked quizzically at her husband but his frown told her that it was her turn to be patient for an explanation.

Terry took a deeper, and rather painful, breath and got started on his explanation. It all came out in one go but he spoke quietly, sounding weak, and it was punctuated by many stops for tea.

"Mainly I've been away since we last met but I've been back here for a little while to get some business sorted out. I'll fill you in later about all that stuff; it doesn't matter for now. I decided to have a Chinese from my local for dinner and took a stroll down a road I know well, or at least, I used to know it. Maybe it's changed." Terry seemed to drift off for a moment but quickly got back in control and carried on. "I came out of the take-away and, before I knew what was going on, I was being pulled into an alley along the road. Then I just remember pain. I was being punched, I fell over, then there was kicking. I yelled for help. I asked why. They kicked me more. It seemed completely senseless."

Terry winced again as he remembered what had happened. He kept faltering while he was talking. It was a slow process but Sue and Jeff were so transfixed they weren't going to do anything to interrupt.

"Then they grabbed me off the ground and yanked me up by one arm. There was this bloke next to us. I don't think he'd been kicking me. He seemed separate from the others somehow. No-one else had said anything but he seemed to know what was going on. Then he started talking.

"'We've not met before, Terry', he started. He sounded better spoken than I had expected, somehow intelligent sounding, given the circumstances. All of a sudden it wasn't senseless – he knew my name.

"'You've taken a bunch of money, Terry. You've got to give it back.'

"'Wha'?' I asked, not even sure of the English language. None of this made sense. Then one of the others punched me again in the ribs. They had hurt before but suddenly it was worse. I started coughing, which hurt even more.

"'Come on, Terry, be smart. Friends of ours know you're the one who's taken their money and they want it back. We know you don't live this kind of life normally so I'll be clear. Make sure it happens the way it should, Terry, or we'll do a lot worse to you than this. You've made things all twistifuddled. You'd best put the money back where it should be. You don't want us to make you all twistifuddled, do you?'

"Then it was all over. As quick as it had started, they disappeared. I sat there for a bit, don't ask me how long, and then stumbled back to my place. At some point I stopped thinking about how much I hurt and started trying to work out what the hell had just happened and, like you asked, why.

"Getting home took ages so I had lots of time to think, but none of it made sense. What money? I go past a bus stop on the way and there was an ad for some beer or other. I don't know why I even noticed it. You would have thought my mind had enough to worry about, but it just made me think back to our conversation when I retired. It's weird how one random thing connects to another in your head. Then a whole bunch of things linked together and I got straight into my car and drove over here. Is there any chance of another cup of tea?"

Sue got up and took Terry's mug over to the kettle. She didn't know exactly what was being said or how it related to her but all of this, and Jeff's serious demeanour, was enough to tell her that there must be a link.

Tea recharged, Terry carried on.

"You remember what I said?" he asked, looking at Jeff. "'Follow the money.' I had that serious look through all the code before I left, especially the new bits that that arrogant arsehole brought in after he took over the IT department. I found the changed code and realised what it meant. At the time all I wanted to do was get as far away from the Teatherstone-Fox bunch of bastards as possible," Terry's feelings towards his ex-bosses were still so full of hate he practically spat their name out as he said it, "so I wasn't interested in doing anything about what I found. I decided that things would probably be as they should be if I gave just enough information to someone I trusted to do something sensible with it."

Sue suddenly realised that there can be a light bulb moment, when everything makes sense and all the bits of information come together to make a recognisable pattern. Jeff still looked perplexed.

Terry carried on. "The rest is clear. You obviously took me seriously: the Teatherstone-Fox Group is still going, so you clearly didn't go to the police; and TF has lost a bunch of money and thinks it must have been me. I guess I can kind of see their point, based on me leaving at the right time, so they got some thugs together to get it back and I got beat up. Cheers."

"Did he use that exact word?" Jeff finally broke his silence when he was sure Terry had finished.

"Which word?" Terry was confused. Surely the main crux of the story he'd just told was not the use of the English language.

"Twistifuddled. Did he use that exact word?"

"Yes, it was pretty unmistakable, but I don't see…"

"Never mind. It's not important. The question is what do we do now?"

"I'll tell you what. All I want right now is some painkillers and sleep. Can we finish this tomorrow?"

"Of course," Sue replied.

She had been quiet for most of this conversation; it had been a lot to take in and clearly the others knew more than her at that time. This would have to change, but she realised that nothing more was going to happen until the rest and pain relief happened. None of them had eaten dinner but even that didn't seem important just then.

As Jeff helped Terry first to the bathroom and then to the spare room, Terry winced with every step but he was so grateful for the chance to lie down he kept his moans as quiet as possible. He didn't bother getting undressed, just lay on top of the duvet and was asleep before Jeff had turned off the main light and shut the door.

*

"We can't just disappear and leave him in this state," Jeff argued, having gone back to his wife who'd been stressing while cleaning up the kitchen.

On his way back downstairs he'd had time to think about the heated discussion he knew was about to happen.

They both kept their voices quiet so they didn't risk waking Terry, although they probably didn't have to worry.

"These people are using violence to get their money back!" Sue's tone was equally quiet, but the strength of her feeling was very evident to her husband. She'd always had this way of making her displeasure obvious through her demeanour and her words, without needing to raise her volume. "Do I really have to state the obvious?" Her time spent cleaning the kitchen had been spent thinking all these revelations through, trying to make some kind of sense of them and coming to what seemed to her to be some very obvious and dark conclusions. She didn't understand Jeff's apparent unwillingness to follow their original plan. "We're not just talking about prison here. We're talking about injury, pain and possible – scratch that, probable – death!"

"They think it's all Terry."

"And what if they followed him here? This makes no sense to me. Why are you being so casual about this?" Sue was starting to lose her ability to stay calm. The tone in her voice was taking on a new nuance – in addition to the confusion there was now fear. All the possible ramifications were getting stronger in her mind minute by minute.

"I checked with Terry on the way up just now. He knows they disappeared sharpish after they beat him up. They wouldn't have wanted to get caught by the police if they turned up. And he's convinced he wasn't followed here. There is no connection to us. At the end of the day," Jeff continued, "this is our fault. A good man is lying upstairs hurting because of our actions."

"I know." The turmoil in Sue's head reminded her of another facet to the confusion. "We can't just leave him, but…" She trailed off in a cross between feeling she shouldn't have to explain the 'but' and general confusion. Was this unwillingness to leave an uncharacteristic arrogance? Or was he right? Was there something else she was missing?

Despite Sue's reservations they decided they had to stay at least one more day, but neither of them slept well that night.

17

"Morning boss." Rob stood at Jeff's office door and cheerfully welcomed him to another day by offering him a cup of tea.

"Oh, cheers," Jeff took the mug gratefully, "I need that."

"Busy night?" The dirty grin on Rob's face gave away his assumption about what Jeff and Sue had been doing the previous night. Jeff was no fan of assumptions – current events were proving that they could be very dangerous – but this time he was grateful for Rob's acceptance of Jeff's silence, meaning his assumption must be right.

"Shall we get started?" Jeff suggested between sips of the still very hot tea. He had a lot of other IT manager-style work to do that day but his desire to keep control of Rob's investigation was going to override everything. "I'd better just check my email first, then I'm all yours," he said, while he used the computer they were both working on to log into his account.

Jeff should have known better. When something is going well, as he had always lectured his staff, stop. If it's anywhere near the end of the day, go home. Do not look for more work. The Law of Sod is a powerful thing, even more so in IT. Something is bound to come up that will ruin any smugness you were feeling about things going so well. What nobody else knew, especially not Rob, was just how unwell things were going at that moment. Or how much things being well depended on Jeff's ability to oversee Rob's work.

Every month the IT department had to make sure the senior management, who may have been hated but still ran the place, got all the business information they needed to do just that. It was an irritating task but it did have one great advantage, at least as far as Jeff was concerned. The business information report included the takings from all the different parts of Cuthbert's, including the highly relevant financial products' direct debits, which meant Jeff could keep an eye on how much money the Teatherstone-Fox Group should be, and crucially was, getting.

Of course, in any normal situation the two numbers would be the same. The number of products sold, times the amount per product, minus all the various costs, should equal the total taken. One of Jeff's jobs from the very beginning of the scam was to make sure this always looked right, so the Teatherstone-Fox Group didn't get suspicious.

When he logged on, the first email in his inbox, complete with red exclamation mark setting the importance as high, was:

To: Jeff Mead
From: John Teatherstone-Fox
Subject: URGENT: BUSINESS INFORMATION ERROR!
Jeff

Last month's business information report showed an unexplained result in the overall takings for the financial products.

Get this sorted.

John Teatherstone-Fox

Teatherstone-Fox Group Director

TF's brusque manner had become commonplace these days and this time he hadn't even bothered with the standard Teatherstone-Fox banner. Normally the lack of useful information in the email would have prompted a lot of investigation into what the problem was before Jeff could even get towards solving it. This time Jeff knew exactly what was going on, and it answered one question that had been bugging him since Saturday. It had never been clear why TF and co. had suddenly got wind of the missing money and got Rob involved. Somehow the wrong, or technically the right, information had got onto the report and into the wrong hands.

A few things suddenly made more sense and needed to be dealt with urgently, but some things still did not make sense. The email made it clear that TF Senior had worked out that the problem came from the Cuthbert's part of the business. Had something only just shown this up? Or did he know straight away and try to disguise it by telling Rob to look everywhere? There seemed to be more questions than answers and Jeff needed more information. All these questions got formed, re-formed and answered and new questions half-formed in another of those infuriating split seconds.

AAARRRGGGG! – breathe – be calm were, in the end, the most coherent thoughts going through his head in that moment.

Jeff quickly got his composure back and looked up at Rob. "Something's come up. More accurately, nothing important has come up but our idiot bosses think it's important and if I don't deal with it now there'll be hell to pay. Can you cope on your own for a bit?"

"You're all right, mate. We did enough yesterday for me to be able to find my way around. Don't worry, I know exactly where you're coming from; I've had enough bosses with no sense of priority."

"You said it."

Jeff hoped he was convincingly casual and didn't show the fact that he knew he was suddenly in a hideous situation. He had been genuinely confident about being able to control the direction Rob went in, as long as he could work with him, and as long as none of the other things that were happening happened. If only.

*

8.51pm

Sue's morning probably felt even worse, but not because of panic over having to deal with unexpected problems. Her problem was not having anything important to deal with, leaving her mind time to stress over what was happening with no control over anything.

She spent the entire morning dealing with the unnecessary hassle caused by her sudden disappearance, and stressing about Terry. Francesca had sent emails all over the place bemoaning the fact that Sue wasn't there to provide the service centre's end-of-month reports. Much like everyone else, Sue was supposed to provide information on the department's activity. It had all been in Francesca's inbox, but in her rush Sue hadn't named it following the proper Teatherstone-Fox Group format, so Francesca hadn't recognised it and went into a panic. Sue spent an unnecessary amount of time emailing various people and making sure they had the right information. Luckily the information wasn't time critical so nothing was really hurt, and it was made a lot easier by the fact that Francesca happened not to be there.

*

Tuesday – 9.09am

Jeff had spent the morning trying to find out why TF had much more information than he should.

It wasn't until 1pm that he found the problem. Over the past six years he'd been very careful about regularly checking his various personal logs to make sure that no-one saw his bit of altered code, and crucially that the correct misinformation was sent up to TF.

That particular month, it just so happened that Cuthbert's report had been compiled and delivered on the previous Thursday afternoon by close of play, as dictated by the central finance controllers. Of course, for all their 'I'm the boss so just do it' style, demanding the report on time, they didn't actually look at it until the next day, the day he and Sue had suddenly disappeared to Switzerland.

Something else wasn't right. As soon as the report was compiled, without fail Jeff had gone through the relevant finances. He had checked that the correct portion of the money, his favourite pasta sauce, was diverted and diverted again into his holding bank. He had checked that TF's portion was going off after that first diversion into their account. And, just as importantly, he had made very sure that the business information report showed what TF expected to see. There had never been a problem but he slept better knowing that when the report was delivered, the expected takings were shown to be the same as the real takings minus the relevant diversions.

Over six and a half years, to be precise, seventy-eight reports had shown the misinformation he wanted. Why was this one different? Jeff stared at his screen for quite a few minutes, trying to work it out. Maybe it was the programmer in him, but he was convinced the answer had to be somewhere in the code.

He went to the loo, made a fresh cup of tea and tried desperately to work out what had changed. He looked through the window to the office Rob was working in but didn't want to start another conversation with him just then. If Rob was doing OK, Jeff going in would be a waste of what was suddenly much needed time. If there were any problems, the time spent away from the real problem would have to go right up, and Jeff wasn't confident of his ability to make a made-up reason for him having to be elsewhere sound convincing.

Rob seemed to be beavering away fine so Jeff carried on back towards his office, still thinking about why this thing was happening.

The report, normally with the correct incorrect information on it, had been sent to the accountants the previous Thursday, the end of that particular month. When the whole scam had started, the whole accounting set-up of the company was in a state of flux because the TF Group was bringing in its own way of dealing with the finances. This had helped Sue and Jeff hide their part of the process. Or at least the change of staff studying the trends, and the change in the format of information provided, meant that no-one spotted the change in the money coming in.

The report would have been seen by a relatively junior staff member first, who collated the different reports from the different companies within the TF Group. Then they would send it to more senior accountants, who looked at the bigger picture, and they would have plugged it into their own spreadsheet, which compared all the individual bits of information with each other and, crucially, with the previous amounts. The financial people seemed to live and die by the trends in receipts, so they had all sorts of pretty graphs showing whether takings were going up or down and by how much. That would have happened on Friday. The fact that that individual piece had suddenly jumped up by nearly a million quid may or may not have been noticed until Friday afternoon.

They would have given TF Senior a brief summary of the whole group's trends at the end of the day, which almost certainly would have included that unexpected jump. Of course, if TF wasn't so involved in the original scam it wouldn't have meant anything to him. He might have just put it down to successful marketing improving the sales or something. But he was, so it did.

The crucial thing was that TF Senior must have failed to notice exactly where the jump was at first. Maybe he wanted more control and brought Rob in the next day before knowing enough. Or maybe he knew straight away and tried to disguise it by telling Rob to look everywhere. But why did he bring an external person into it at all? He knew very well he was breaking the law. Jeff realised his brain had asked some of those questions already, but it was starting to spin out of control. More questions.

This entire thought process only lasted the time it took Jeff to walk the ten yards between the office Rob was in and his own, but it at least explained one part of the puzzle. He got to his door and, despite the sudden stress, couldn't help smiling a little at the thought of TF Senior having a minor heart attack when he saw the jump in that particular number.

*

Tuesday – 2.03pm

Sue had dealt with Francesca's panic by early afternoon, and the voice in her head worrying over Terry was refusing to be ignored.

She still couldn't leave the office before two, and after the five-minute walk to the bus stop she just missed the direct bus home, which would have taken half an hour. The three minutes she had to wait for the next bus only added to her nervousness. Terry had been sleeping fine when they'd left him that morning but some maternal instinct buried deep inside her worried about him being alone. She tried to fill the time with a text to Jeff to let him know what she was doing but that only took seventeen seconds.

Her mood was not improved by the damp drizzlyness of the day. It wasn't at all heavy, but in their state of stress that morning she hadn't remembered her umbrella and she stood waiting for the bus getting wetter and colder than she could really cope with.

The next bus took her into the main bus station in eight minutes and then she had to wait five minutes for the bus home. At that time the parents hadn't started clogging up the roads picking their kids up from school so the bus journey probably took even less time than normal, but Sue was getting more nervous as time went on, and the perceived journey time seemed to be an age. Normally she didn't pay a lot of attention to the bus journey on the few occasions the car to work wasn't an option. Her brain usually made a choice between still being half asleep, stressing about the day she was about to have or being hacked off about the day she had just had. Of course, she was only human, and occasionally she couldn't help comparing it to her alternative journeys in her other life.

On that day, however, all she could think about was Terry and the perceived torture of that seemingly snail-like journey. The multi-storey car park over the bus station seemed to have too many cars going in or out of it, which was snarling up the roads the bus had to take. If she'd been in a non-obsessed moment, Sue might have wondered if they were people leaving town after a morning's shopping and a lunch, or people coming into town after a morning at work, something she'd done herself. In that moment she just wanted them out of her way. They had no right to be there as far as she was concerned and she was in no mood for questions about hypocrisy.

It didn't help that at every stop there seemed to be a mother with a pram and at least one toddler, not to mention the shopping bags. Sue's imagination was exaggerating the time each of them took, but the time spent juggling everything they had with them meant the whole thing felt painfully slow. There was a broken-down car partly blocking one of the main arterial routes heading towards Sue's area, which slowed the traffic down as two lanes had to merge into one to get round it. The journey was actually taking not much over its usual half hour; it just didn't feel like it.

When she finally got to their closest bus stop, less than an hour after she had left her office, she started almost speed-walking towards the house. By the time she turned into their street the pace had gone from a brisk walk to a trot and she was now running. Her mind was on other things at that moment but in calmer times she would have been quite thankful that she was slim and fit.

*

Tuesday – 2.44pm

Jeff's smile didn't last long.

"You should have let me deal with this!" TF Junior's unmistakable voice, coming from the entrance to the department down the corridor, had that well-known angry tone of exasperated whispering that was far louder than probably intended. He always did have an ability to sound pompous, full of himself, and at the same time not so obviously under his father's thumb. The Teatherstone-Fox family didn't let on much about their relationships, they kept the mere underlings at a cold professional distance, but it had always been clear that TF Senior was in charge. Of course, he hadn't mentioned TF Senior by name but people around the company had heard that tone before and, with the facts Jeff had, it was obvious what was being discussed.

These days it was a blissfully rare voice around the department. He wasn't around the branch office that often. He seemed to spend most of his time either at head office, producing dictates from afar, or sunning himself in Spain.

"If you remember," again with more exasperation, "I'd only just got away and I was getting into what promised to be a very lucrative deal..." – probably a euphemism for a poker game with rich ex-pats – "If you'd phoned me straight away I could have come back earlier and checked out why this has happened and dealt with it directly!"

By this point in the conversation TF Junior had reached his office and unlocked the door; he was the only one in the department who made sure no-one else could use his office, so he rushed in and firmly shut the door behind him.

Jeff knew exactly what he was doing in there. The weekend's events suddenly made a lot more sense. TF Senior had discovered what was happening on Friday, contacted Rob to start a legal investigation and Terry's attackers to do a much less legal version. It must have seriously angered him to know that he didn't have the control he expected over the situation. All of this without first talking to Junior, who probably would have pointed out the blatantly obvious point that if they weren't very careful, Rob could discover their end of the scam. So he had rushed back from Spain to prevent that from happening. TF Senior may have felt that he should have mastery over this but clearly Junior understood the ramifications much better. There was a family dynamic there that Jeff did not have time to worry about.

Then he suddenly remembered how long it had been since he had heard that voice. Last Friday, when he had left in a hurry after an urgent text from Sue, he'd almost collided into Junior on his way out. Junior had obviously been preoccupied and had barely taken any notice of how pathetic Jeff's made-up excuse had been.

Of course, that same day he was distracted by the sudden call to Switzerland and had forgotten about the encounter, and about the business information report.

Jeff went into his own office and, more gently, closed the door. He went straight to the computer and his private log which allowed him to see the activity around the critical parts of the software. Sure enough, there it was, and it explained everything. That night TF Junior had replaced the version of those critical bits of code with a new version that didn't include Jeff's extra bits. That meant that it was only TF's bit of the scam that was missing from the report and not Jeff's.

Not quite everything was explained; Jeff still didn't know why Junior had made this change, but frankly he no longer cared. He just had to make sure Rob didn't find all this out.

And then he got the text:

'Home. Now!'

*

2.48pm

With every step Sue became more angry at herself for leaving Terry alone to cope with all his injuries, and she had started having fearful thoughts about his ability to breathe. She had no real reason for worrying about that aspect of his injuries but something was stuck in her mind and it kept getting worse.

As she turned into their road, at nearly the farthest point from their house, her run was getting faster. As it was a dead straight road, and even though the street light was still off at their end, she could just about make out their front yard in the mid-afternoon light. All of their professional neighbours were at work, so Sue and Jeff's were the only inside lights turned on. As she got halfway down the road she realised she could make out her neighbour's evergreen azalea. It being December, there were no flowers, but she could see the full shiny green leaves.

This wasn't right. The sun was still up at nearly three o'clock, but it had been a particularly grim overcast day and there wasn't much light at their end of the road. They'd never felt the need for their own outdoor lighting over their front door. By then the drizzle had stopped but everything was still wet and shiny where there was light to reflect off it. But at the end of their road there shouldn't have been any light. There was no way she should be able to see those azalea leaves so well. Somehow some light was reflecting off them.

It was only when she reached her house that she realised the light was coming from inside her own front door. The door was open and letting light out of their hallway over both her and her neighbour's front yards.

She tore through the open front door, calling out.
"Terry?!"

It didn't take her long to see he wasn't there. She rushed around their house checking every room, calling as she went. She fast ran out of hope and had to work hard at not panicking. She realised, just as fast as she moved, that it wasn't only that she didn't know where he was, she had no information to even start trying to work it out. In any normal situation that would have driven her nuts, but this in no way resembled normal. Given the odd bits of his behaviour over the last couple of days, Jeff obviously knew more than she, so she quickly sent him a text that got the urgency of the situation across as quickly as possible.

"Home. Now!"

18

3.10pm

By that time the school rush had started so Jeff's journey home took an infuriating half hour, which gave Sue a chance to look around the house to try and glean some more information.

The front door didn't look like it had been broken open but when she got to the back door, it obviously had. It had just as good a lock as the front door, and of course it was connected to their alarm system. There was only a simple wooden gate to the passage leading to the back of the house so they had made sure, they thought, that the security was still tight at the back door. The alarm hadn't been set while Terry was there and the workday quietness had obviously given someone the chance to make all the noise they wanted. Brute force had been enough to break the locks and get into the house.

Sue went straight upstairs to where she had last seen Terry sleeping and saw that the bed looked slept on. The bathroom had obviously been used again but it looked like Terry had at least tried to clean up afterwards. There was still a smear of blood on the sink and the shower had been used. That couldn't have been easy in Terry's state, and there were lots of hand marks where he had obviously had to steady himself.

When she went back downstairs she noticed there was half a cup of very cold tea and a half eaten piece of toast neatly placed on the dining table. She realised she had run so quickly past the front door she hadn't paid much attention to the yard. When she went back out she saw their gravelled yard was not as flat as normal. It looked like several sets of feet had kicked it into a mess.

In her amateur detective mode she suspected that someone, or more likely some people, had broken into the back, and Terry had rushed out of the front door and been caught by someone else waiting there. It didn't really matter how this had happened. The important fact was that Terry wasn't there and clearly not by choice.

What was missing was any evidence of who had been involved. There was nothing to tell her who these people were or, crucially, where Terry was now. The time Jeff was taking to get back gave Sue time to start stewing over those assurances that nobody knew Terry had made his way to their supposedly anonymous house.

*

3.42pm

"It's OK, I know where he is," Jeff stated with little doubt in his voice when he got home and Sue had explained what she'd found.

"What?!" Sue replied, confused and getting more and more annoyed at the fact that there were clearly a lot of things Jeff hadn't shared with her. After a moment's thought and with a bitter edge to her voice, she asked, "Do we have time now for you to explain all of the things you know and I should know but don't?"

Jeff sighed. "It wasn't deliberate, I promise. A lot of things suddenly make sense and I should have talked it through earlier, but what can I say? In answer to your question, no, we don't know how long they've had him. I promise I'll do better when there's time."

"OK, do what you have to do, and I'll get angry at you later. While you're gone I'll get things ready for us to leave." There was something in Sue's tone that her husband knew meant there was no arguing over the 'leave' part of that statement.

Before he left, Jeff went upstairs to the bedroom, opened the wardrobe and moved his trainers and the boots he kept for outdoor or DIY work out of the way to get a small bag from the back of the top shelf. He hadn't used it since he was a kid but something had told him it might come in useful one day. Then he quickly changed into jeans, a T-shirt, a warm fleecy jacket and the trainers, and went to their car.

The school rush was finishing so it was a fairly quick twenty-minute drive to the pub where he had picked up the fake passports. It was one of those 'family-friendly' open-all-day pubs that looked cheerful and friendly, had a colourful plastic slide outside and was managed by an equally friendly man with connections none of the families knew about.

He went straight to the manager, who was tidying up, getting ready for the early evening rush, and had a quiet word so none of the families could hear. The manager's eyebrow raised as Jeff walked up, and it was clear he knew the passport supplier very well, knowing things that only a close contact would know. The publican seemed to believe Jeff when he stated that someone's life was in danger unless he could find him urgently.

The house was only a ten-minute drive from the pub on another quiet residential road. It was well past four when he pulled up, and the sky was very dark. Unlike his own road, all of the street lamps were working so Jeff could clearly see that most of the houses had a fairly new family-style car in their beautifully paved driveways. There were a few four-wheel drive cars sitting outside. It may have been an unfair stereotype but Jeff couldn't help assuming that they were probably driven by so-called yummy mummies, with the kids in the back. Of course, none of the cars were parked in the two-car garages attached to the houses. That could have been down to laziness or showing off, but clearly there was a nice bit of money here. Most of the properties were quite nicely sized four- or five-bedroom detached houses with well-tended plants around the front. Jeff's dislike of assumptions was forgotten as he imagined those yummy mummies having time to tend the gardens. He told himself off for not thinking in the modern age and, perhaps more importantly just then, for not concentrating on the job in hand.

The house he was interested in was slightly smaller but also a very nice modern-looking detached place with a garage and no car in the drive. Unlike the other houses there wasn't any planting in front. Everything looked neat and tidied away. The only exception was the one large front window on the ground floor with a curtain only three-quarters drawn. The front door was in the middle of the building, obviously leading into a porch, with the garage on the far side. Upstairs there were two square windows either side of one thin window which sat over the front door. The window over the garage had fully drawn curtains, shown by the lighting inside. The other window was completely dark, with a dull light coming from the narrow middle window. Having spent time house-hunting, Jeff knew enough about how standard houses at the nicer end of the housing market were to be able to imagine the internal layout.

The only light Jeff could see was from the downstairs front room, the lights changing colour and flashing in a way that suggested a TV was being watched. He guessed that it had three bedrooms and a bathroom upstairs and that Terry was probably in one of them. Once he felt he had worked out everything he could by looking, he got out of the car. He had a brief thought about crime paying very nicely, and then he remembered his own situation and smiled slightly.

He walked as casually as he could towards the house, mindful that there were people around and he wanted to appear as normal and unremarkable as possible. Of all the things he had learned over the last few years, the most important was the need to look as if he belonged wherever he was.

The garden gate was on the nearest side of the house and not locked, so he easily opened it and walked down the side path. The back door was locked and luckily the light shining from next door's kitchen gave him enough to see by.

He took the package he had retrieved from the wardrobe out of his jacket pocket and hoped his old skills hadn't left him.

*

3.51pm

As soon as the front door had shut behind Jeff, Sue went to the cupboard under the stairs and lifted out the vacuum cleaner and the mop and bucket behind it. She picked up the two smart overnight bags from the back and took them to the dining table. She opened them one after the other and checked that everything was there that would allow herself and Jeff to become Jennifer and Mark forever.

The change of clothes, the passports, the driving licences, everything that they immediately needed was there. She had no idea how long Jeff would be but as soon as he arrived they would be ready to leave. She knew there was the small matter of how they were going to get Terry safe but at that moment she had to concentrate on the practical tasks to stop her brain from exploding. She didn't want to waste time but she made herself do everything slowly and methodically so nothing was forgotten.

A voice in the back of her head was in the process of rehearsing the enormous row she wanted to have with Jeff, and it was getting louder. She tried so hard to concentrate on whether the right paperwork was ready for them, but all she could think about was that voice angrily saying:

"*It's only obvious NOW that you recognised something in Terry's story?*"

She went upstairs to the spare room to check there was nothing there that they would need.

"*We always promised each other COMPLETE honesty. Even before we were married we knew how important it was. Oh yes, and COMMUNICATION. Remember that promise?*"

She got the laptop out of its locked drawer and looked around her until she was satisfied that that was the only thing that needed to go with them.

"*So, please explain how MY husband could keep so much from me that affects MY liberty, MY safety.*"

While she was upstairs she went into their bedroom and changed out of her work skirt and heeled shoes and into much more comfortable jeans and flat shoes. She went back down to the kitchen and started tidying up the stuff Terry had obviously used in preparing his tea and toast.

It had been hard enough to keep that voice quiet while she was doing things that required thought, but the mundane tasks like doing dishes made it impossible. What made the voice worse was having to deal with whatever had happened to Terry. She found a role of gaffer tape under the kitchen sink and tried to patch up the damage done to the lock and the surrounding wood in the back door. She also grabbed one of the bricks they had lying around in the back yard. When she came back inside she put it on the floor just inside the door to keep it shut.

"*Yes, I know it's all supposed to be about US, dear, but you seem to have ignored that little detail when deciding what information to share.*"

What really hacked her off, if she was truly honest with herself, was that this whole thing had been her idea in the first place. All those years ago she was the one who suggested they played the Teatherstone-Fox Group at their own game, yet somehow Jeff was the one with more control.

The doorbell interrupted her thoughts and the jobs she was doing – and her heart for a moment. Her heart was getting a bit fed up of having that done to it. She stared towards the front door, almost expecting to be able to see straight through it for an explanation of this totally unreasonable noise. She felt a combination of fear and indignation. She put the mug she'd been washing into the sink, dried her hands on the Welsh-print tea towel, went back into the dining room and threw the two smart overnight bags into the back corner of the room where she hoped they wouldn't be seen.

*

4.15pm

Jeff had been quite a good lock picker when he was in the care home, which had come in very useful when the gang he was in wanted to sneak out of and back into the home late at night. He had convinced one of the older boys to teach him the knack of lock picking. Something about the technical art fascinated him. He loved the fact that he had learned how a bit of the world worked and then learned how to make it do what he wanted. It may have been because it was dark the very first time he learn to pick a lock so it was always very natural to him. All the other types of locks he'd picked when they were out and about helped him learn more. The situations they had got themselves into had taught him to become faster and quieter than anyone else, even his original teacher. Some of the others could do it but no-one was ever as fast as him.

Luckily, as he felt each of the pins move and was finally able to turn the cylinder, he discovered he did still know how to do it. He had to take his gloves off to feel everything fully, which was not that comfortable on a chilly day. The process took a lot longer than it used to but he was relieved to know he still had the skills. Halfway through, next door obviously finished what they were doing in the kitchen and turned the light off. Having to finish off in complete darkness was annoying but by that point he'd got back into the swing of it and was able to finish blind. Using long unused feelings he put the tools back in their bag and into his pocket and he carefully stood up.

He could still hear the TV blaring out from the living room, far louder than it needed to be, and he couldn't see anything happening in the darkened kitchen through the textured glass. After standing still for several seconds longer, just to be sure there was no noise or movement he couldn't explain, he opened the door as gently and as quietly as he could. He silently and carefully stepped up the few inches into the kitchen. There was just enough light seeping in from the front rooms to be able to navigate the kitchen units without bashing into any furniture. It was obviously too early for dinner preparations so the kitchen was tidy and he could easily walk between the counter and what looked like a breakfast bar without touching anything. There were stools neatly tucked in around the bar but they were easily avoidable. He could tell the flooring was some kind of nice laminate, which was a relief. He had been worried about his trainers making the annoying squeaking noise they made on his cheaper uneven flooring.

He carefully made his way into the hard-floored hallway leading alongside the stairway and towards the front door. The other thing that helped mask any potential disturbance he made was the noise coming from the front room. Clearly several people were watching some afternoon quiz show, and every now and then a gruff male voice would yell out the answer to a question as though the TV contestant could hear him. Jeff was fairly sure these were the men who had beaten up Terry, so the first time he heard a deep voice, whic sounded like it belonged to a very large body, yelling out, he nearly turned tail and ran.

"It was Leonardo DiCaprio, you stupid cow!"

It was everything Jeff could do not to laugh out loud.

"No, you moron!" yelled out an even rougher and bigger sounding voice. "Ewan McGregor was in *Moulin Rouge!*"

Jeff decided not to waste time wondering how such a rough-sounding man knew about a costume musical, which he himself had enjoyed far more than he'd let on. He was actually grateful for the ensuing argument, which acted as cover for any noise he made walking along the darkened hallway and up the wide stairs.

Everywhere had the same laminate flooring and he had to be careful of the pictures hanging on the stairway wall; he was far too focused on his mission to pay them any attention but even in the semi-darkness with the hall light off he could subconsciously tell they were well chosen. Something about their framing and mounting looked like they cost a bit.

When he got to the top of the stairs the floor was still the same laminate and the roughly square landing had more pictures on some of the walls. Low-power lights came out of two wall fittings on either side of the landing, which had added to the dim light coming up the stairs. Quickly spotting four closed doors in each of the walls, he tried the first door on his left, which he knew led to a room over the garage. It was locked.

"Oi! Sod off!" yelled a disembodied, clearly angry and slightly familiar voice coming from an echoey room. "I told you this was going to be a long one. Go use the bog downstairs!"

*

4.11pm

Sue opened the door and Nicholas Teatherstone-Fox announced, "I need to see Jeff."

There wasn't any anger in his voice, just unequivocal instruction. He almost sounded like someone who was used to not being argued with. Even through the confused panic rising in Sue's mind she thought she perceived a tiny quiver of doubt in his voice.

What on earth is he doing here? How did he find us? Oh yeah. The IT boss would have access to people's personal details. I need to get rid of him FAST. Jeff could come home at any moment with Terry in whatever state. What does he know? What are we going to do with Terry when they get back? Focus! We'll deal with that later.

"He's not in," Sue replied with equal strength. She made sure her voice had no clue of uncertainty in it.

There was 0.94 of a second between TF Junior's opening pronouncement and Sue's factually correct reply, which was enough time for Sue's mind to race through what felt like an hour's worth of thoughts. Her one argument with Jeff became many arguments with herself, while her face stayed completely impassive.

"It's urgent."

I suppose this could be useful. As long as he's here we've got some control over him. It's a risk. Can I really pull it off? I could find out what he knows. Does it really matter? I've just got to get out of here as soon as I can. I have to get rid of him.

"I've no idea how long he'll be, but you can wait here if you want." *WHAT! Don't stress it. You can do this.*

Sue stepped back, allowing him to come into the hallway, keeping her composure and a serious but emotionless expression. He accepted the invitation. His expression, Sue felt, was some combination of angry-looking seriousness and snobbishness. *You're making assumptions. Stick to the facts.*

"Take a seat," she said, directing him into the living room. "Would you like a tea or coffee?" *Politeness helps.*

"Tea. Please." There was definitely a gap between the answer and what seemed to be treated as an expected but unnecessary politeness. "Milk, no sugar," he added as if barking an order.

Sue was glad of the time on her own in the kitchen making the two teas, glad of the time to get her thoughts in order and carefully plan out how she would run the conversation.

AAARRRGGGG!!!!!

4.21pm

Jeff wasted no time and went straight to the door on the other side of the stairway. It opened into a semi-dark bedroom with a window over the road, and the light coming from the street light outside was just enough for him to see the room was empty. The next room was also empty, apart from a pool table and a couple of old-fashioned arcade video game machines. *Finally*, Jeff quickly thought as he quietly closed the door, *something that looks like it might belong to men who would beat someone up.*

The fourth door also opened into a much darker bedroom that overlooked the back garden, and again the landing light gave him just enough to see that at the end of the double bed was a chair with someone sitting in it. It seemed like the person's head was slumped to one side. As Jeff was stood there he suddenly saw two slight glimmers in the middle of the head, as though the light was reflecting off suddenly opened eyes that looked straight at him. The arms were slightly unnaturally placed, exactly following the line of the chair's arms. His legs were also splayed apart and seemed pinned to the front legs of the chair. It could have been a woman sitting there but Jeff instantly knew it was the slim-built Terry.

Jeff took a split second to use the light from the landing to take in the layout of the room, even the rough-looking rug underneath the chair. As soon as Terry's position was fixed in his mind he slipped into the room and shut the door behind him. The grimness of the day meant there was no light coming in from the back window so the room was now completely dark. Luckily, another part of Jeff's childhood still came in useful. During those secret excursions out of the care home he got very used to creeping through pitch-black rooms. He still knew how to work out and memorise a room's layout when there was light and then translate that into careful movement when there was none. He felt his way along the nearest wall until he got to the point he knew would be parallel to Terry, then he carefully stepped across the empty part of the room between the wall and the chair.

He knew how many of his steps it would take to get to the chair and then he turned, reached into his jacket pocket and took out the bag with the lock-picking tools. He also kept a sturdy pair of clippers in it, which often came in useful. Still in complete darkness, he found them by touch, took them out and found and cut the tie around Terry's nearest ankle, being careful not to cut Terry. He did the same to his other ankle and then reached up to Terry's wrists to free them.

Terry slowly tried to stand up, pushing against the chair arms to overcome the stiffness caused by sitting in a forced position for several hours and some more beating he'd been given. He sat straight down again when his leg felt unsteady but the second attempt worked better, with Jeff's help. Jeff moved round and supported him on his far side so that Terry could hold onto the wall.

He was very glad of Terry's slim build as they slowly shuffled along the wall towards the door. When they got to the door Jeff gave Terry a gentle squeeze to indicate that he wanted to pause there. The pain of the squeeze made

Terry wince but he managed to do it silently. This was going to hurt, but getting away from there was better than the alternative.

Jeff strained to hear if there was any noise outside the room but all he could hear was the same level of yelling at the TV downstairs. He could tell the door must still be closed, and there was nothing coming from the man spending so much time in the upstairs loo.

*

4.17pm

Sue chose the cheapest tea they had from the back of the cupboard, unwilling to spend any more of her own money than she had to on that man. Then she chose a much nicer one for herself. When the teas were ready she waited for a moment, took a deep breath and then took them into the living room.

Nicholas was sitting looking incredibly uncomfortable on one of their most comfortable armchairs. When they first bought the house they'd chosen the type of chair they could sink into. Not so much they couldn't get out of it but definitely comfy. They were just big enough so the two of them could have a very close cuddle. Nicholas wasn't a particularly small man, about five feet ten, and he was slim built, so when he tried to sit straight in the chair, unwilling to relax, he looked ridiculous.

Sue put his tea on the little side table next to him. Even putting a mug straight into his hands seemed too much like contact to her. She took hers to the other armchair, wondering if he ever lowered himself to drink tea out of a mug. Just to make a point about their relative comfort in her house she tucked her legs up under herself.

*

4.23pm

Jeff reached across Terry, very slightly opened the door and peered through the narrow crack to confirm the upstairs landing was clear. As soon as there was more light, it became apparent that Terry's mouth was covered over by a wide piece of gaffer tape and there was drying blood around his badly bruised eyes and nose. They couldn't move as fast as Jeff really would have liked to at that moment, and a quick glance into Terry's eyes was enough to confirm that they didn't have time to deal with the gaffer tape.

Jeff gently opened the door enough for him to lead Terry out and they began to squeeze through. They moved sideways, with Jeff leading and Terry resting his free arm on the door frame. As soon as they were through Jeff reached back and pulled the door shut. They moved across the landing as quietly as possible but Terry was still stiff and shuffling more than walking so nothing was as quiet as they needed.

"Whoever's out there, put the kettle on. I'm nearly done in here," the disembodied voice from the echoey bathroom yelled.

Terry's eyes went wide, or at least as wide as they could with all the fresh bruising, showing his sudden terror. Jeff held his free hand out with a gently calming motion and they carried on towards the stairs. It was a painful and annoyingly slow process but they managed to find a technique for getting down the stairs. Jeff's free hand felt the wall as they went down, carefully avoiding the pictures; he took as much of Terry's weight as he could with his other arm and Terry used the banister for more support. They knew that at any time one of the quiz show watchers or the bathroom user could stop what they were doing and discover them. There was nothing they could do except keep going, so they did, one step at a time.

When they finally got to the bottom Jeff led them straight to the front door. There was another door leading to the porch that needed to be negotiated but by that point they had developed a workable technique so this didn't cause them too much of a problem. The front door was the type that easily opened from the inside so Jeff gave Terry his first breath of fresh air in hours. With timing that wouldn't have been out of place in a slapstick comedy film, they stepped out of the house just as they heard the upstairs loo flush.

*

4.19pm

"Are you going to tell me what you want to talk to my husband about?" Sue asked, taking control of the conversation.

"No," he answered decisively.

"Don't you think I'll understand?"

Maybe Sue's question was so obvious to him he didn't think it warranted an answer. There was often an intrinsic assumption that anything to do with IT would not, or perhaps could not, be understood by non-IT people. Jeff knew it just bored her near to death but she was plenty intelligent enough to understand it. Junior may have thought less of her. Maybe other thoughts were on his mind. Who knew? And frankly, according to Sue, who cared?

"You don't like me, do you?" he suddenly said after some time.

Sue smiled a little into her tea and after a bit of thought answered, "Do you really care?"

He didn't answer straight away so Sue decided it was a good time-filler and carried on, being careful not to babble or drag it out too obviously.

"I can't say I really know you. The same is true of your sister. I see your business sides but nothing else." The way he had treated Gina told her a bit more about him than she was letting on but she wanted to avoid veering into the inevitable rant.

She drank some more tea, noticing that Nicholas's was being ignored. This gave her the advantage of having a probably quite obvious but convenient delaying tactic, and he was left looking awkward.

She knew the answer she really wanted to give but that rant would have been unhelpful and she needed to keep better control than that. She couldn't even let herself think the things she was really feeling in case they showed in her voice.

"From a work point of view it must be very obvious that we don't agree with the way you've run the business."

"Why do you stay, then?" Nicholas asked, with a tone that strongly suggested he didn't understand why anyone would act differently. Sue didn't know if he had never cared or had just assumed everyone knew his version of the truth.

"When I started working for Cuthbert's," she answered, "it was a wonderfully caring place to be, where we all looked out for each other, and the company's success came out of working together."

"It sounds lovely but doomed to fail."

"In which case it had been 'failing' for over 170 years, and I never got the impression that the Teatherstone-Fox Group would have taken over a company that wasn't making good money. To answer your question, I still care deeply about the people who've worked at Cuthbert's for many years and I want to do my best to protect them against what you are doing."

"We are just operating a modern successful company and maximising the output of all available resources."

"Do you actually believe that management-speak?" She knew from Jeff's reports that he didn't normally talk like that. He may be an objectionable person but he was a practical IT man and the words didn't sound quite right being repeated by him.

"You obviously don't understand how modern businesses operate."

Sue had trouble keeping herself calm whenever anyone started talking like that but another sip of tea helped her keep the unhelpful language she actually wanted to use out of her question. She'd get back to that line of questioning if she needed to waste more time.

"I know exactly what you're about. Making money. For you. What else is there?" She didn't bother waiting for an answer. "Do I like you? No. Do I like what you've done to Cuthbert's? No. Do I think you care what I think? Definitely not. Do I care what you think? Even less so." She kept it all very matter of fact, answering each question without showing any of the hatred she truly felt.

She carried on in the same measured way. "People have lost their jobs. People have left because they felt they had no choice. All so you can make more money. You, and of course your father and sister, have absolutely no regard for anything but yourselves."

"Outsourcing is *the* best way to run a company in today's world," he authoritatively stated, again repeating the tired old management-speak he'd picked up from his father and sister.

"And there it is," Sue responded with amusement. "The famous 'O' word. Out-jobbing. Out-skilling. Out-experiencing. Out-caring. Out…"

"Actually, all of those things are provided in a much more cost-efficient way by a well-chosen external contractor. You only have to look at the…"

"Do not interrupt me in *my* house," Sue ordered, having to work incredibly hard at not losing control of herself. Many conversations with Francesca had taught her how to deal with interrupters by not becoming that rude herself. Only this time she felt it was important enough to act in kind. "We are not at work now and you are not my boss here. What I was going to go on to say was that all of those benefits have been shipped out to someone else who does not truly understand our business. No matter what you say you will never convince me that the products and services we provide to our customers are any better than they were before the 'O' word was brought in. In fact, I have presented plenty of evidence to show that they are actually worse. Provable facts, which I have presented to your sister, and I have been totally ignored."

"I'm sure all the important facts have been duly considered," Nicholas responded, having recovered from being slapped into place, a happening he was clearly not used to.

"I know very well that they haven't. At the beginning you started off using lots of lovely words about listening to us, and a few of us were foolish enough to believe you, but now you don't normally bother. I was a bit surprised when Francesca asked me to write the report on how outsourcing would fit the service centre. I'd thought the model was to be applied across the board."

"The out-sourcing model has not been applied to all departments, only those where there are real benefits."

"You actually believe that, don't you? Do you ever relax from making money?"

For the first time since he arrived Nicholas smiled. Not a very genuine-looking or broad smile, more of a snide, rather weak-looking half smile.

"That's what life is about, isn't it?" he offered as a self-assured sounding explanation.

Sue would have considered pitying someone with such a narrow outlook, if she didn't know what she did about him. Then she half smiled to herself, knowing what she did about her own behaviour over the past few years. Then it struck her. *HE KNOWS!*

Suddenly there was a scraping noise from the kitchen. Nicholas looked intrigued but Sue knew that it was the brick holding the broken back door closed being pushed across the floor.

"I'll go see to that," she said abruptly without further explanation, and left the living room, closing the door as she did so.

As she suspected, when she got to the kitchen Jeff was in the process of shutting the door again with the brick.

"I saw TF Junior's car and wanted to come in quietly the back way."

Sue looked over Jeff's messed up and slightly bloody appearance.

"That didn't work. I take it Terry's in hospital?"

Jeff nodded.

With a look on her face that left no doubt, she continued, "Oh, and by the way, he knows."

As soon as Jeff and Terry had started driving away from the house, Jeff had made it clear he wasn't accepting any argument about taking Terry straight to the nearest Accident and Emergency department. As they were driving, Jeff didn't say much else about what was going on. There didn't seem much point. It was only when he pulled up as close as he could to the A&E entrance that he turned and said:

"I'm so sorry this happened to you. You really don't deserve it."

"Don't stress it. If I hadn't been in such a hurry to get away from Cuthbert's I'd have done exactly what you've been doing."

They parted with a well-meant handshake, which made Terry wince some more, then he slowly hobbled into A&E,

trying to work out how he was going to explain his state without police involvement. Jeff went straight home and, after his quiet discussion with Sue, went upstairs to get changed.

Sue went back into the living room.

"Jeff'll be down in a few minutes. He got messed up looking after a sick friend."

Nicholas's raised eyebrow suggested he didn't quite believe her but at that time she really didn't care.

"It sounded like you had to struggle with something out there," he responded.

"It wasn't a problem. I was thinking about your earlier question, about whether I like you." Sue was very aware that they both knew they were playing a game, but she had to delay dealing with the real problem for as long as possible. Her main advantage was that she was fairly sure he still thought of her as being less than she was.

"Actually, I was wrong in my earlier statement. I do know a bit about you outside of work, and what I know makes me like you even less."

"I wait with baited breath to hear what you think you know," he said with an amused arrogance in his voice.

"The way you treated Gina was nothing short of disgusting."

"Who?"

"Well, that reconfirms my idea about your character. The previous service centre manager. My previous boss, before your sister took over."

His face still showed no signs of recognition so she continued, "You tried, badly from what I understand, to crack on to her. You tried several times, with your skills in this field never improving, and when she finally convinced you she wasn't interested you made sure she didn't get the job that was rightfully hers."

"I do remember now. She needed to be replaced because she wasn't very good at her job."

"That is complete bullshit!" That did it. Sue could keep her composure under all of the rest of the stress, but a friend being so completely lied about was more than she could take. Her anger was the first emotion she had ever showed him because it was too strong to be held back. "She was brilliant at her job, knew the business inside out, and you punished her because she bruised your deluded ego." *Calm. I can't afford to lose it right now. Breathe.*

"It became obvious that we could not work together," he said, looking much more amused than he had any right to be.

"You are quite right there," she responded, managing to regain control over herself, "but there is no way she should have been punished for your actions. I still don't understand why you care what I think of you," Sue said, making another move in the game. "Surely I'm just another worker. There to help you get what you want. I'd have thought my feelings were irrelevant." She thought of a few more insulting words than 'worker' but she wanted to stay logical and calm-headed, so she avoided words like 'grunt', 'stooge', 'monkey' and 'dolt', even though she was sure that was what he thought.

Nicholas was still doing his best to look like he was sitting straight in the armchair whilst looking down on Sue. Sue stared straight at him as she talked and again thought she saw a slight change in his demeanour while he considered her comment. The snobbery his face showed almost imperceptibly changed to a moment of doubt. Did he actually care? Even though he must know what's going on?

Chosing her words carefully, while trying not to make them sound chosen, Sue continued:

"I guess the real crux of the question I've spent far too much time asking myself over the last few years is, 'Why are you like you are?' Whenever we've met, and from comments Jeff's made, you seem to try to be like your family, but it doesn't quite sound right coming from you. When you try, it sounds like you're overcompensating for something or other." Sue raised one eyebrow in a sense of irony. "Not that any of it sounds right to me. Why are you behaving like you are? The charitable part of me thinks you could do better. So, why don't you?"

In a voice that to the uninitiated sounded just as snobbish as before, but to Sue sounded just a tiny bit doubting, he said, "Good questions all. Maybe we have more in common than you think. Maybe I'm not the person you think I..."

Of course, it was at that moment that the door opened and a cleaned-up Jeff strode into the room.

"What is going on, Nicholas?" Jeff sounded angry even though he worked hard at not shouting. "What right have you got to be here?"

Nicholas stood up, without any of the grace he would have liked, and faced Jeff. "I was just having a very nice chat with your wife. She obviously worked out very early on that I know what you have been doing, and she's been doing a passably skilful job at keeping me distracted until you got home." Clearly any chance of digging into motives and behaviours had disappeared, and the boss-like demeanour had come back to full swing.

"Look," Jeff said, already getting impatient with TF Junior's tone, "it's been a difficult day and I really don't have the time, the patience or, in fact, the energy for this. Will you please just…"

"You are stealing my money and I want it back," Nicholas announced calmly, matter-of-factly and with all the authority he normally showed.

"Excuse me?"

"You what?" Sue and Jeff both responded at the same time. They didn't look at each other but both hoped that their confused outbursts sounded convincing.

Jeff's thoughts were suddenly racing. *Will denial sound convincing? Does he know that I know about his theft? He must do. He can't report me to the police. Can we do a deal? Do I want to do a deal with him? I thought they thought it was Terry? How did he work it out? FOCUS!*

"You come to my house," Jeff responded, having regained his composure, "and start throwing around accusations out of nowhere. What on earth do you think gives you that right?"

"I'll grant you I did make one schoolboy error in assuming my track-covering was good enough. I put my changes in a place where nobody goes. At least that's what I thought. For years everything seemed as it should be. Then last week I had to make some changes and everything went wrong. Or maybe it went right. More right than before, anyway. Things hadn't been right for ages but we only just noticed. Nice work, by the way."

Nicholas looked a lot more comfortable and in control as he explained himself.

"I was annoyed at being called back from a very lucrative holiday," he continued, "but once I returned to the office and started going through the routines I quite got into the challenge. Of course, I had to dig out the stuff from before I'd made last week's changes, and it took a bit of digging to find your changes, but it all made sense once I did."

All of this was addressed to Jeff, with Sue more or less ignored by Nicholas. She decided to let this be, because she realised there could actually be an advantage to observing from outside the conversation. By that time, Jeff had walked further into the room. From his quick assessment of the room he saw the way Nicholas had obviously felt uncomfortable on the slouchy chair, and how much more control he clearly felt standing up, adversarially facing him, so Jeff took a seat on the end of the sofa. Nicholas was obviously a bit put out by this display of comfort but he sat back down anyway.

"What do you want?" Jeff decided not to mess about anymore but still kept everything very businesslike. Sue was still sitting on her chair, observing.

"I told you. I want my money back!" Nicholas was starting to look a little amused, almost as though he were enjoying the chess game.

"You've obviously decided that two people living in a small urban house must be instantly able to provide this money you say you want."

"My father doesn't agree with me. He thinks some old ex-employee must have done this, but I know it has to be you, and quite frankly I don't care how you're hiding it – I want it back."

Sue started feeling like this game was getting silly. He obviously knew what had been going on and she didn't see any point in pretending any longer.

"My question is, why do you think we should return it?" she asserted into the conversation.

"Because it's mine. That seems obvious to me." Nicholas looked as though he thought this was a ridiculous question.

"That's debatable. You stole money from Cuthbert's takings. Some of that money strictly belongs to Her Majesty's Revenue and Customs. Not to mention the profit shares staff members should have got, before you canned the scheme that is."

"So?" he answered.

"So if we've done what you are accusing us of, which I'm not sure I can admit to, you are just as guilty as we are. Exactly what power do you believe you have to instruct us to return anything?"

"Oh, is this the classic 'if we go down, you go down with us' routine?"

"No, it's the 'who do you think you are to tell us what to do?' routine. You have no power here."

"Actually I do. My father knows people who can make your lives very uncomfortable. It's not my style, and so far this has all been quite civilised, but if I don't produce a result by reasoned argument he will not be happy. His background left him with contacts I don't really want to know about but he will use them if you don't give back what should be ours."

"Everything will become all twistifuddled," Jeff said under his breath.

"What?" Nicholas asked.

"Nothing," Jeff answered with barely disguised anger in his voice. "Now you're threatening us. I want you to leave." He got up and opened the living room door.

"OK," he said as he got up, still far more awkwardly than someone making a threat wanted to. "Just so you know, I've told my father all about my findings and I know he has already spoken to his contacts. They will be in touch."

"Leave! Now!" Jeff's tone didn't need volume to make the strength of his feelings obvious.

"Fine," Nicholas said as he brushed past Jeff and went straight out of the front door.

Sue and Jeff looked at each other, knowing that the conversation they needed to have was going to have to wait even longer.

19

Jeff went straight to the laptop to get it ready for them to leave. Because he had always had the internet router in place, he knew that that was the only locating beacon linked to them, so he could safely grab the laptop and take it with them. He regularly did sensible things, like deleting cookies, so the whole thing was safe.

There was just one little thing he had to do first.

The conversation with TF Junior had made it very obvious that taking his money wasn't enough. As soon as Junior left, Sue made it very clear that he deserved to be left with as much blame as possible, so he made sure the set of files he'd been keeping safe were ready to use.

Ever since their discussions when they were discovering how evil the Teatherstone-Fox plans were, Jeff had been storing away the information that would prove the TF involvement in the original scam. He'd stored the original audit file and a copy of the specific routines that showed the original change in the code that diverted the takings, and who had made it; that photo of the TF family with the 'independent' financial auditor; and the log he'd made of the business changes the TF Group had made in their time.

He'd also made a careful log of the TF history and the various companies they had done the same to. It had all been sitting in his private directory waiting for the right time. The day's events had also crystallised the hatred they both felt and the realisation that his plan would go a long way to making sure the people in the wrong got what they deserved.

The other detail he had to take care of was a quick swap of software routines. Right from the beginning he had kept this change ready to quickly slip into place whenever they decided to go. TF's original scam had diverted the money – Jeff smiled as he remembered his pasta sauce analogy – and immediately afterwards Jeff had re-diverted it to his own account. The next simple little change was to do his diversion first. It would only be for that month. It wasn't as good as he would have liked – he would have liked to have truly cleaned them out – but at least it would mean that Jennifer and Mark's account got the whole £5 million (and change). It had gone up over the past six and a half years, so was not just the measly £900,000 they started with. He kind of hoped Rob wouldn't look at that particular part of the system while he made the change but it was all about to come out anyway so it didn't matter too much.

It only took a few minutes to get the email ready to send to Rob, and in the meantime Sue got everything ready to grab so they could finally leave, and even managed to start a note she wanted to leave. They'd both been very calm and businesslike about the jobs left to do but there was no hanging about, so Sue was even more inwardly stressed when the doorbell rang.

"I think you have something of mine," a very well-dressed man said from the porch as she opened the door and saw Mark standing in front of her. "You must be my sister-in-law."

*

On any other day Sue might have been startled to see this man clothed from head to toe in Armani smiling at her. The shoes, the jeans, the striped shirt, even the watch and cufflinks were exactly what Jeff's alter ego wore. The hair was styled differently to how Mark would have done it, a bit shorter and gelled upwards, and his nose seemed to bend slightly differently to one side. It was still odd to see a man who looked so much like Mark in front of her usual home.

"Joe, I presume," Sue said and stood back to allow Jeff's identical twin brother to step into the house.

Surprisingly early on in their relationship, when they realised it was right enough to quickly feel real trust, Sue had known that Joe existed. Jeff had only told her a bit about his early life. It was so different from the life he had made for himself that he preferred to leave it in the past. He did, however, tell her about Joe. A twin was hard to forget no matter how hard he tried to split away.

He had told her the bare bones of the split, which had started with one particularly nasty incident that had always stuck in Jeff's mind.

Joe had effectively become the leader of the group that Jeff helped sneak out at night. It didn't get that way through any show of force or by debunking any previous leader, he just had a way of being able to convince the others he should be listened to and followed. There were six of them, still under or around ten, but Joe had a slightly older outlook on life and gave the impression, true or otherwise, that he understood the bigger picture. Even at that age, before he knew that the word existed, he had a certain charisma.

When they were younger he was the one who told Jeff to break into their school's tuck shop so they could steal their favourite sweets. He was the one who convinced them to ration the amount they stole, and not to sit there stuffing themselves until they were sick, so it wasn't too obvious what had happened. He was also the one who organised the use of the sweets as some kind of currency around the home. Jeff found himself regularly paid with his favourite sweets for doing the less intelligent or lazier kids' homework. There must have been something thin in his DNA because it seemed a miracle he never put weight on.

By the time the brothers got to twelve, Joe was getting bored of sweets and was becoming more ambitious, so the breaking-in got more serious. He used his growing charisma to convince his brother to get them into people's houses. One of the other kids would have been told to check out suitable targets after school. The obvious choices were places where the owners were clearly away and didn't have alarms or clever security systems. Joe was very firm that none of them should ever bunk off school. He knew that minor crimes would more quickly get blamed on kids who broke the rules in other ways, so they had to do their best not to stand out.

That was why it all went bad in Jeff's head and why the thoughts of breaking away started. One of the other gang members, a slightly younger kid called Robbie, started messing about in the year below them at school. He stopped handing homework in, even though Jeff had helped him out, and even started missing classes he didn't like. The school's headmaster started keeping an eye on him and had a conversation with the home's staff, so they were keeping an eye on him as well. Which meant, as Joe realised, that they were keeping an eye on the rest of them as well. Lucrative night-time outings had to stop and Joe was not happy.

Joe was a smart lad and he did not let his unhappiness flare out in any kind of outpouring of temper, as again he knew this would bring unwanted attention in his direction. By that point he really knew how to control the other lads and decided that Robbie had to be taught a lesson. He had to be taught that his, Joe's, way of doing things was the best way there was. Again, to avoid getting any attention in his direction and using those persuasive skills, he got two of the other boys to teach that lesson. Harry and Lee had already grown slightly bigger than the others and were known to have a bit of a temper on them. Joe convinced them to take Robbie aside after school one day and give him enough of a beating to teach him that he was going the wrong way – by Joe's definition, anyway. He made sure they understood that it had to be hard enough to get the message across but not so heavy that the damage was too obvious and more questions would be asked.

He even invented a new word to describe the painful twistedness he wanted Robbie to be in and the state of confused befuddledness he expected the slightly dim-witted lad to be in until he worked out why he was being hit. After that none of them ever stepped out of line again and Joe cemented his authority. 'Twistifuddled' became his favourite word whenever he decided that threats or violent actions were needed, provided of course by someone else.

The only person not scared or impressed by Joe's behaviour was his own brother. Jeff was horrified by the way Joe had used his undeserved power to force other kids to do his dirty work, and how he used violence, by proxy, to control people. He started making excuses to avoid going out with them. Suddenly he often became very sickly, getting lots of colds, the flu, even pretend hurt legs. He taught one of the other boys how to pick locks so he was no longer needed. He was aware that that meant he was helping someone else learn to break the law according to Joe's directions, but he knew it was his only way out of that life.

Both brothers used their brains to suit their own ends: Joe to use other people to his advantage, and Jeff to get educated and start a different life, eventually in IT. Unusually, Joe didn't seem to worry about this loss of control over one of the group; there was an unspoken agreement between them to stay out of each other's lives and not cause the other trouble.

Sue had never wanted to know any more details and it was a part of his life Jeff was glad to break contact with. At that moment she knew their hope of disappearing silently had gone and her best action was to keep a close eye on what was going on, making sure she had as much information as possible.

"Jeff," she called up the stairs with a remarkably light matter-of-fact voice as they walked along the hallway, "your brother's here!"

Jeff was about to finish the email to Rob, explaining everything, when he heard the doorbell and, within seconds, Sue's call. He pressed send and two seconds later was at the bottom of the stairs to see Sue indicating towards the living room where she had obviously left Joe.

She went in first, leaving him a moment to breathe and get calm before he followed her.

As soon as all three of them were in the living room Joe looked straight at his brother, while Jeff had deliberately left the door open.

"You left blood on my bannister; very untidy," Joe said, used to being in control and speaking first. "Where is he?"

"I'm surprised you care anymore," Jeff responded. "Teatherstone-Fox Junior must have told you who he thinks really took their money."

The four sentences spoken in the living room, and a little previously held information, gave Sue enough to understand what was going on. She vaguely knew that the passports their alter egos used had come from Jeff's childhood contacts but hadn't pressed the point at the time. It was only Joe's appearance on their doorstep that suddenly made it clear that they had held Terry. Obviously that meant they had beat him up in the first place, and Jeff had clearly recognised something in Terry's recounting that meant he knew this. The connection to TF Senior was the only missing information just then, but compared to the current situation it really didn't matter.

"How've ya been, bruv?" Joe asked in an affected way, putting on a turn of phrase he'd never used before. "You're not looking quite as well dressed as I would have expected,

227

given what, as you quite rightly pointed out, I have been told about you."

"That just goes to show the problems assumptions can cause. I do recognise Armani, though. You're obviously doing pretty well for yourself in whatever work you've got into."

Joe bowed slightly, his vanity unable to avoid enjoying the compliment. His natural arrogance was impossible to miss as the three of them stood facing each other. Jeff kept his position near the door, arms hanging down, making sure he was ready for whatever happened, and Sue stood with her arms folded, not looking at all impressed with the situation. Joe looked arrogantly relaxed, with his legs slightly apart and one hand in his jeans pocket, looking as cocky as he obviously always had.

"You always did manage to stay looking smart while you got everyone else filthy doing whatever you wanted." Jeff looked at his brother, partly amused, partly judgemental. "That's part of what made me decide to get out of that life. I didn't want to be one of your tools. I could see exactly where that could lead."

"Leading is just a talent I seem to have ended up with. Style is an extra goodie," Joe replied. "Actually, right now I'm a bit annoyed with myself," Joe continued as he took in the comfortable décor in the living room. "I mean, I didn't think too much about the passports you bought from me however many years ago. You weren't forthcoming with an explanation and I didn't ask. Mind you, when Mr Fox asked me to get my colleagues to talk to his ex-employee yesterday I didn't know there was a connection to you. So maybe I shouldn't judge myself too harshly.

"I didn't even recognise the address when my colleagues followed him, painfully slowly, and even when we all came to pick him up this afternoon I didn't question who might live here. I have to say you were very good when you got him. I mean, I obviously heard you trying the bathroom door but you got him out without anybody noticing. Impressive. It was only when I saw the blood on the bannister that I knew what the noises had really been. And after we'd gone to so much trouble convincing him of the error of his ways, or so we thought. Of course, the guys did the heavy work in the bathroom so we didn't get blood on the carpet."

"I take it you didn't know it was me until TF Junior got the message through."

"Actually, no. It did look a bit suspicious when we checked the state of the back door and saw the scratches you'd caused picking the lock. It made me smile at the time because we could see clear fingermarks around the lock, and I remembered my brother never did wear gloves."

"With gloves on I couldn't feel the tumblers properly to get my speed up."

"You were very proud of that speed, for a while, but that wasn't really it either. Yes, Mr Fox told me I'd find what he was looking for here but he only gave me your first names. He was never any good at remembering people's names so really it was only when I got here and Sue answered the door that it all came together."

"We've never met," Sue said, coming into the conversation for the first time.

"Don't forget I've seen your passport picture," Joe responded. "Your turn, bruv; how did you work out that Terry's disappearance was to do with me?"

"I wasn't the only one to leave telltales. As soon as Terry told me you threatened to make him all 'twistifuddled' I instantly recognised your favourite phrase from when we were kids."

Sue's impatience started to get the better of her. "This is all lovely and fills in lots of blanks but clearly you're just wasting time until your 'colleagues' get here." She continued, "Frankly I've no interest in being here to have the shit beaten out of me until I give back this money you still haven't proved we have."

"Yes, well, they could be a while. Perhaps foolishly I sent them off to Terry's place and came here on my own. I rang them as soon as Mr Fox's son came out and confirmed that what I was looking for was here. Given that it's rush hour they probably got stuck in traffic. Either way it's OK. I have all sorts of conversations ready to talk through. I'm sure there's more to be said on what made Jeff go straight and me, well, slightly less straight, to take up even more time. If that fails, there's the philosophical difference between what you're doing and what I do. Are you really what they call 'good people'?"

Unable to resist the invitation to tackle the subject of conversation between him and Sue many times over the last few years, Jeff responded, "That's a very good question but you need to define your terms. We did spend a bit of time right back at the beginning worrying about whether we could define ourselves as good. In the end we just settled for 'better'. We didn't need to spend much time on whether we were better than the TF clan. Robin Hood kind of sorts that one out, ish. Yes, we're enjoying what we've got but we've made sure the only people getting hurt deserve it.

"You and me, 'bruv', that was harder. Then I remembered why I decided I wanted nothing more to do with you and your way of doing things."

"Do tell."

"Sue and I were going to do this ourselves. If it all went wrong we were the ones who were going to suffer."

The look Sue shot him made it obvious how unimpressed she was with the time this speech was taking, and the disregard for the, admittedly thin layer of, discretion left. Jeff understood the look but once he had started this explanation he realised that these were things he'd always wanted, and just now needed, to say. He found it almost impossible to stop.

"You were always so spotless, in every way. You had this knack of getting other people to do anything that would be messy, in any way. You always looked smart and you never got close to anything that would make you look less than *perfect*. You also made sure nothing would directly get you in trouble. Remember Robbie? You weren't even there when he got taught his lesson about bunking off school. The blood and the blame was on other people. There was no justice. I hated that."

"Actually I did get messed up once. You may notice my nose isn't as straight as it used to be. A few years after you disappeared, a rather lucrative enterprise of mine trod on other people's toes a bit and they took exception to that. They went straight for me and my lovely straight nose. Of course, that only strengthened my determination to be more careful about keeping myself safe. Thinking about it, I do wonder where you got that love for that version of justice," Joe pondered, doing a not very subtle job of trying to extend the conversation as long as possible.

Jeff caught the look on Sue's face that clearly told him not to even think about starting down that path.

He responded with a simple, "I guess we'll never know."

Sue got fed up of being ignored and with the length of time all this was taking. "So, what's to stop us hitting you over the head and getting out before your colleagues turn up?"

"Jeff wouldn't do that to his own brother and you're not strong enough. I think I'm safe. You're what, five feet three? Jeff and I are both six feet and..."

As Sue sprang forward on her left leg, dropped her arms and brought her right knee up into very hard contact with Joe's testicles, he discovered exactly how little Sue appreciated being patronised like that.

She was slightly surprised at how much his reaction seemed to live up to every stereotype of a man being hit like this but her knee definitely met its very tender mark. As his knees buckled under him and he ended up kneeling on the floor, he lost the ability to breathe. The self-defence class Sue had gone to after the handbag incident in Italy was another old skill that got remembered on that day. This time, instead of trying to escape the situation, she had used every ounce of strength she had to head straight in. She had showed him that she may be small but she knew how to use what strength she did have.

Before Joe had a chance to recover, her right fist caught his nose with an equally well-placed upper cut, sending his balance completely off, and he started falling sideways towards the floor. She was very glad of the other lesson, about always keeping her thumb on the outside of her fist, because the feeling of his nose breaking hurt her hand enough.

While Joe was still trying to catch himself against the floor, Jeff crossed the gap between them, grabbed him from behind and pulled his shoulders backwards. In very short time he was forcibly laid on the floor with his legs bent under him and his nose still bloody from Sue's punch. From underneath the blood Jeff could see the confusion on his brother's face. Jeff was able to move around, sit astride his chest and keep Joe pinned to the floor.

"Now who's all twistifuddled?" Jeff asked, feeling a little bitter about it having to be like this but satisfied at the turn of events.

Sue ran into the kitchen, found the gaffer tape she'd used on the back door and ran back to the living room. As she ran she bit the edge of the tape and tore six inches of it free of the roll.

By the time she got back Joe had recovered the power of speech, if not movement. Jeff was lying forward across Joe's head and holding his arms against the floor. Joe's bloody face was pointing sideways towards the room's door.

"Get the fuck off me, you…" Joe clearly wasn't used to being the messed-up one and it almost sounded as though anger was tinged with indignance.

That first piece of tape went straight over Joe's mouth, reducing his yelling to wide-eyed grunts. Sue wrapped some more of the tape around his wrists, using several layers to make sure they were incapable of being freed without a blade. Then Jeff shifted his weight so they could roll Joe onto his side, and they did the same to his ankles. Jeff got off and pulled Joe over towards the fireplace. He was certainly not going easily, and it was all Jeff could do to control his kicking legs enough to avoid getting those smart Armani shoes in his back.

The strange thing was that they'd never behaved like this before. Jeff had taken himself out of Joe's world before he was ever made to get violent, and Sue had only had a few self-defence classes, years ago. Maybe they'd paid more attention to the action films they'd watched than they realised. Whatever the reason, they had him tied up and rendered helpless in less than thirty seconds.

Once Jeff had pulled Joe far enough towards the fireplace, he pulled Joe's arms up to the lovely vintage ironwork and Sue used some more of the tape to bind his wrists to the grating. Checking the sturdiness of her handiwork she did take a moment to be a little amused by the blood that had dripped over his Armani shirt and was still dripping over her soon to be ex-carpet.

20

To: Rob

From: Jeff

Subject: What you're looking for

Attachments: mod log.doc; orig sw.pdf; new sw.pdf; auditor pic.jpg; TF history.doc

I'm sorry for telling you like this, you deserve so much better, but this will show why I really don't have time for the explanation you deserve.

I've attached a bunch of files that prove it's actually the Teatherstone-Fox Group that started the scam you're looking for. They'll show you how it was done and should give you all the legal evidence you need to make sure they get what they deserve.

Yes, I know that these files also prove that Sue and I have been doing the same, but if you've been listening to us for all these years you'll know why they deserve to be caught more than we do.

It turns out that they've got 'friends' who are more worrying than getting caught by you.

You and Kat have meant so much to both of us but click here to: Reply, Reply to all, or Forward

Rob had just been getting ready to pack up for the day. Professional pride meant he wanted to do a good job and beat the challenge; on the other hand, he wasn't paid enough to work long hours. He'd shut down the software he'd been looking through, frustrated that he still hadn't found any sniff of missing money, and did a last check of his Hotmail account. Not much he wasn't expecting, but just before he was about to shut it down Jeff's email came in.

Nothing made sense at first. The email left him confused but curious enough to forget about going home. When he opened up the software files he found that someone, he assumed Jeff, had helpfully highlighted lines of code which looked very wrong. It didn't take him long to work out the important facts, and while re-reading Jeff's email suddenly a switch flicked in his brain that sent him from slightly amused at his best friend's cleverness to terrified for his best friend's safety.

Shutting his Hotmail account down was a split-second job but then he grabbed his coat and ran to his car, not caring about the state he left the Cuthbert's computer in.

He didn't know if the traffic was actually worse than normal or if it was just his stress levels making it seem that way, but the trip over to Sue and Jeff's seemed to take an age. When he finally got to their street a lot of the other inhabitants had got home from work and he couldn't park nearly as close as he wanted. He sprinted half the length of the street and his stress levels went even higher when he realised that their front door wasn't closed properly.

"JEFF! SUE!" he called out. Nothing.

The living room door was open and at first glance the room seemed as normal, but his second look showed the blood on the carpet and some cut gaffer tape attached to the fireplace.

His instant reaction was to get his phone out to ring the police but he needed more information first. He went into the dining room, which actually looked very tidy. There was a single sheet of A4 paper on the table held down by an unopened bottle of beer.

Thoroughly confused, he went over to the table, moved the bottle of his favourite real ale away and picked up the paper.

In Sue's writing it said:

We will miss you and Kat.
Please forgive us.
X
PS The coloured glasses are not tat - enjoy.

Rob sat down on the nearest chair, looked again at the bottle of beer, leaned back and let out an enormous laugh. He got it.

EPILOGUE

May – a year and a half later

"At least tell me we're going to get a chance to see the cathedral while we're here!" Kat yelled to her husband as he speed-walked towards Milan's Malpensa Airport taxi rank ahead of her. "It was built over 600 years ago, according to the guidebook."

As Rob reached the nearest taxi and started to open the rear door he turned back towards Kat. "I promise there will be tourist time, but you know what we came here for."

As Kat reached and started to get into the taxi, handing her overnight bag to Rob, she carried on, "Yes, but think of it this way: if we don't look like typical tourists while we're at it, it's going to look a bit bloody obvious to anyone watching. And I fully intend to do some clothes shopping while we're in the fashion capital of the world."

Rob grinned to himself as he got in. He gave the taxi driver a piece of paper with the name of the hotel they were staying in written on it. It was the only way to avoid the confusion that would be caused by his shockingly bad attempts at Italian. "And yes, I know our first stop involves ice cream. I wouldn't dare try to prevent that."

"That would probably be an MLM, a Marriage Limiting Move. Or at least," she continued more quietly, "an SLM," not feeling the need to translate that acronym.

*

December – a year and a half earlier

As soon as Rob finished his very fine ale at Sue and Jeff's dining table he searched the cupboards and found the coloured glasses. They were very pretty but he didn't get what was so special about them so he left them in the cupboard.

He looked around the rest of the house – everything looked fairly normal. Someone had obviously messed up the spare bed, and when he looked closely he realised there were bits of blood in the bathroom and on discarded clothes. He didn't find anything in the office, except an open desk drawer with nothing in it.

Going back downstairs he discovered the broken state of the back door and realised his friends had disappeared leaving an unprotected house. That made him change his mind about the glass set. He found a bag in the bedroom cupboard and some newspaper from the kitchen and carefully put the glassware – *which may or may not be worth anything,* he thought – into the bag.

He grabbed the note from the table and left everything else pretty much as it had been, before heading home for a difficult conversation with Kat.

As soon as Rob got home he forwarded the email from Jeff to one of his contacts in the police fraud department. He wrote a bit of an explanation to go with it, aimed at a fraud expert who was only missing the specific background. Of course, he worded it to point more at the Teatherstone-Fox Group and as little as possible at his friend. They weren't idiots, Jeff would not avoid his share of blame, but hopefully they would concentrate on the big guys first.

Rob knew he had to get that business out of the way first because once the conversation with Kat started the shock of the whole situation would start setting in. She had been recovering from her own long day with a cup of tea and the paper in their kitchen.

"What's up?" she asked, when he sat at their breakfast bar. Something in his demeanour didn't seem right.

"Good question," he responded. "Short question. I get the feeling it's going to have a very long answer. We may have just lost our best friends."

"What?! What's wrong with them?"

"Oh no, don't worry, it seems they're alive and well," he said, realising quickly that he had chosen his words badly. He knew he couldn't be absolutely certain of that fact but he needed to explain the situation fully before tackling Jeff and Sue's current state.

The conversation was long, as Rob explained what he knew and how it looked. His training as a cop and his IT mind, his ability to analyse the world in a logical way, completely left him when he started talking about his best friend. It had all made sense earlier. Now he rambled

240

backwards and forwards between when he knew, what it must mean and what he didn't know.

When he finally came to a rest, both of them sat in silence taking it all in.

Kat was the first to break the silence.

"So, if I've got this right, what you are saying is that two people we have known for years, and thought we knew well, have been stealing money for some, as yet unknown, time and now they've disappeared. Is that right?"

"Put much better than I could have done, and yes, that's exactly what I'm saying."

"I don't know about you but this might make more, or at least some, sense if we eat. Let's get something in the microwave."

Rob nodded and got a packaged meal out of the freezer. Normally they ate much better than that, preferring freshly prepared food or their own leftovers to frozen, but that evening they just wanted food that didn't need thinking about.

Once they'd eaten, they started questioning everything they knew, or more commonly didn't know, about their friends.

"I guess the main question now is 'Where are they?'" Rob eventually said after they had moved to the living room with a bottle of wine.

"Actually, I'd start with 'Are they OK?'," Kat said.

Over the following month everything changed but neither of those questions got answered.

The police of course investigated the Teatherstone-Fox family and their 'friends'. Within a very short time John and Nicholas Teatherstone-Fox were arrested for the fraud they'd pulled on Cuthbert's and further investigations started on their previous companies. Francesca Teatherstone-Fox was arrested for involvement after the fact, given that there was no proof she was directly involved, but she had most definitely benefited from the profits. Their tame auditor was also arrested, for tax evasion and false accounting. Tax evasion was also going to add to the Teatherstone-Fox family indictment. These could add up to long custodial sentences for all involved.

Once he had recovered from his beatings, Terry made all the necessary arrangements to spend the rest of his life travelling. His house sold for a decent amount so he made sure he could leave forever.

Rob had never known about Terry or Joe, so they were never bothered again. Even though they had no good feelings towards each other, Jeff clearly couldn't drop his own brother in with the police, so Joe was let off the hook. He lost his revenue stream from the Foxes but it didn't take him long to find another.

Cuthbert's became a very uncertain place to work for a while. Police and tax officials were all over the place and the company got put into administration while all the various legal issues were dealt with. This took long enough for the non-TF-related senior management to get together and take over the company. In time, many things improved for the staff and the customers, and the entire company was able to head back towards Cuthbert Rigby's original ethos. Above all, a lot of people were re-employed as all of the outsourced work was brought back in-house.

*

Rob and Kat had many discussions over whether they should try and find Sue and Jeff. On the one hand they missed their friends, but on the other they knew the police wanted them and would follow Rob if he got to them first.

Kat did do some internet searching about the decanter and glass set. At a loss as to what it actually was, she just put her best description of it into the search engine. She guessed that if it was actually worth anything the tacky looking goldie bits might actually be gold, so she was a bit surprised when the search:

glass decanter blue gold

actually brought up some pictures of very similar glass sets. She was even more surprised to notice that some of the pictures were accompanied by the word 'Italian', and she nearly dropped the tea mug she was holding when she saw the word 'antique' next to one very similar picture.

As soon as she could, she took one of the glasses, very carefully wrapped up, to a local antiques dealer. A very nice stereotypically old gentleman told her it was indeed an antique. In fact, he very calmly said he thought it was 18th-century Italian glassware and the set could be worth over £10,000. He advised her that it wasn't really his area of expertise and her best bet was to take it to a large auction house on a specialist sale day.

When the two of them made a special trip to just such an auction they were a bit saddened to find that the fact that one of the glasses was broken reduced the value considerably. The £19,000 they did make did, however, was a very nice consolation and Rob promised to never again try and wash dishes when he was drunk.

In a sense Rob was a bit surprised that it was more than a month before they stopped pretending they didn't desperately want to know where Sue and Jeff were. Without even realising what they were doing they started discussing, normally fuelled by Friday evening wine or beer, what clues they might have noticed in things Sue and Jeff had said or done.

Wales was considered a possibility as that was where Sue's mum was. A quick check of the Births, Deaths and Marriages registry was tried to find out where Sue was born, a possible clue to her mum's home. The problem was that the death search actually showed that Sue's mum had been killed at the same time as her dad. This raised many questions about the morals of what Sue and Jeff had done. Sticking it to the TF bunch was one thing, they truly deserved it, but mis-using a loved one's memory like that seemed another level of crime. That took some thinking about but eventually Kat and Rob decided that they'd not judge before they knew all the facts.

Italy was a strong contender as soon as they realised that that was where the glassware was from. When they thought about it more, it seemed to fit in with things Sue and Jeff had talked about and food they liked. A memory triggered in Kat's memory – Sue reciting dinner in flawless Italian – and it all seemed to make sense.

Rob started looking at the timings he knew about, things like when the scam started, so he could try and work out when they must have started going to Italy.

That was where the trail went cold. With another quick search Rob realised there were nearly 60 million people in

Italy, living in nearly 150 cities. And that was just the urban types. That was a fair bet, given how much he knew they loved city life, but the odds of finding them were still not good.

*

May – a year and a half later

"*Due chocolato gelato*, um, please," Rob stiltedly asked the waiter at a street-side *gelateria* near the centre of Milan. The waiter dealt with enough tourists in a day to understand even the worst attempts at ordering and went away to fulfil their order.

"That's *due gelati al ciocolato*, Mr Geek," a familiar male voice said from the next table over.

Rob and Kat twisted so sharply in their seats Kat almost fell off hers.

"So much for looking nonchalant," his female companion added.

It took Rob and Kat a few moments to recover. In that moment the many conversations they had had about how they felt about what Sue and Jeff had done suddenly became irrelevant. In no particular order, they had been proud of what their friends had done to the Teatherstone-Fox criminals, angry that Sue and Jeff had basically done the same, sad that they had lost their best friends, afraid that they could be in danger, angry that they had kept this a secret for so long and, if they were honest, more than a little impressed at the cleverness of the whole thing. At that moment all of that distilled into annoyance that Sue and Jeff had found them so easily and joy at seeing their friends.

"It took us a year and a half to find you," Rob stated in a mixture of those emotions. "How did you manage to find us in a few hours?"

Once she was happy that there was enough chatter all around them to hide what was said, Sue responded first, through a slightly smug grin, "Once we knew when you'd be here it didn't take a genius to work out what Kat's first priority would be. It made sense that you'd aim for the most popular places, so we just came and used our eyes."

"I am a bit impressed you found us at all," Jeff added. "We thought we did a good job of covering our tracks."

"It took some doing – the world's a big place – but there were some clues." He looked at Sue and continued, "You did love cooking your Italian food."

"And let's not forget the glasses," Kat added. "They were a bit of a giveaway."

"Italy is still a big place," Jeff came in. "I'm guessing there was a lot more to it than that."

"True," said Rob, "you were very careful about your computer usage, always a skilful geek. I didn't get to use any of my skills to find you online."

"Yep, it was great," Kat said; "the 'non-geeks' won in the end. Good old-fashioned reasoning and following our noses."

"Hang on a bit, Mrs Smug, I worked out who'd bought the most likely type of flat at about the right time, if you remember."

"Yes, and who went through it all and worked out which purchaser was most likely to be our friends?"

"And who made sure all the web-based investigations…"

"Such as they were."

"Thank you… were done so no-one else could follow our tracks?"

"Oh, how we've missed your bickering," Sue said, enjoying her friends' company. "The Italians know how to argue but none of them have your style."

That evening, over a lovely dinner at Mark and Jennifer's favourite restaurant, Kat suddenly remembered an old question.

"Did you ever come back home after you left?"

"No, why?" Jeff/Mark asked.

"I thought I saw you once near your old house. We went back to grab a few bits before it got sold off by the mortgage company."

"You mean nick a few bits?" Sue/Jennifer sarcastically asked.

"Are you really going to have a go at me? Anyway, I thought I saw you," she said, nodding in Jeff's direction, "sitting in a car down the road."

"I promise it wasn't me," Jeff responded.

"Oh well, it was one of those split-second things where I was only looking out of the corner of my eye. Whoever it was drove off at that moment anyway."

"I think we've both had ghostly moments," Rob added. "We've both been so preoccupied with finding you we've seen things that don't make sense all over the place. I even thought you were at the airport this morning. Daft, I know."

Sue and Jeff looked at each other with matching expressions.

After dinner they said their goodnights. They kissed and hugged with an enthusiasm that Rob and Kat knew meant their friends really were glad to be reunited, and agreed to meet in the morning.

At eleven the next morning Rob and Kat turned up at the apartment block, were let in by the pre-warned security guard and went up. They assumed that the open door was in expectation but found no response when they called out, "Hello!"

*

"*Guten abend*," welcomed Lukas as Rachel and Dave arrived at their central Vienna apartment block.